The Last Time

Nicole Baker

Contents

Chapter One

Charlotte

I stand on the splintered boards of the front porch, looking at the house that used to bring me peace and tranquility. A house that was more than just a home. It was a safe haven. A place where some of my fondest memories were made.

It's in shambles now. Paint chips are scattered along the porch, showing years of deterioration.

That's the funny thing about a home. You have to put time and energy into it to keep it from falling apart. I suppose you can say that this home represents my relationship with my father.

After years of neglect, it's unrecognizable. Its former beauty is hidden so far beneath the surface that you almost don't remember if it ever existed.

It's been a decade since I've set foot on this porch. It's incredible what ten years of vacancy can do to a place. The last time I was here, my life was so much simpler. My parents were still together, and my father was...well, still a father to me.

I still remember the night he left. Although, does anyone really forget a moment like that?

Mom and I were in the kitchen making an apple pie for the end-of-summer party at the marina. We were leaving the following day to head back to Cincinnati before school started up again. I was seventeen and just about to enter my senior year of high school. I was excited to get it over with and graduate. I thought life on the other side was going to be freeing.

How naive I was.

I was helping my mom with the lattice top of the pie crust when Dad appeared by the front door, his suitcase propped up next to his left knee. He said he was just going to go back a day early for work. He used to fly back and forth throughout the summer while I stayed with my mom in a small part of Savannah, Georgia, called Isle of Hope.

I should've known by the look on his face that something was off. Looking back now, Mom knew. She had on a brave face after he walked out the door, but she knew.

When we got back the next day, he served her divorce papers.

Nothing was ever the same again.

Senior year turned out to be nothing like I had pictured it. And it went from bad to worse. It didn't take my father long to find another woman to settle down with and remarry. Sometimes, I wonder if he already found her, and it just took him a while to get the courage to leave us.

Penelope was nice enough in the beginning. She put on a smile for me, faking her excitement when it was my turn to spend the weekend with them. I knew it was all a lie. Her kids were her pride and joy. I was just a nuisance she pretended to care about.

After a while, it was too much effort for her to even fake it. She thought she was subtle with her eye rolls or sighs whenever I asked my father to go somewhere with me.

"Hey, Dad," I'd say. "What do you think about going to a Bengals game this year?"

His face would light up, only to steal a glance at Penelope, who couldn't hide her annoyance.

"Maybe next season, sweetheart."

Luckily, I was old enough to choose who I spent my time with. If my father didn't want me around, then I'd spend the time with friends. But the sting of him consistently choosing his new family over me never went away. Every holiday, birthday, big life event that went unattended by him was another sucker punch to the gut.

You would think after a while, the shock would wear off, but it never did. I stupidly found myself wishing—hoping—for him to come around.

But instead of feeling those feelings of anger and disappointment, I would push it all down. Pretend it never existed. Sometimes pretend *he* never existed. It was easier that way. One gift I had was the ability to tune out the world and my emotions. I'm not saying it was healthy, but it worked for me.

Until now, as I stand face to face with my past.

When I got the news that my dad had passed away, the shock prohibited me from grieving.

How do you grieve the loss of someone that you lost a long time ago?

It was as if I had already mourned the loss of him at seventeen, and my brain didn't know how to mourn a second time.

The funeral was horrible. I watched my stepmom and stepsiblings grieve him appropriately while I stood in the corner feeling like an outsider to their world. Mom was there for moral support, and I suppose because once upon a time, she loved the man.

But the two of us were strangers to him. He didn't know that I worked for the NFL or that my mom recently took up pickleball. He didn't know about my recent heartbreak or that Mom was still struggling financially even a decade after their divorce.

When the lawyer called me to meet him at his office regarding my father's will, I thought it would be to formally tell me there was nothing for me in the will.

When he told me I was left with our family vacation house, I almost fell out of my chair.

My stepmom is fuming over it. Even though she's refused to come here, knowing it was a place that held so many wonderful memories that didn't include her, she still thinks it belongs to her.

She's why the house is in such horrible condition. But from what I overheard one night in the beginning of their marriage, she wouldn't dream of setting foot in a home that he shared with my mother.

Still, she knows it's worth a lot if it just had a little TLC. Which means she wanted it in her name, not mine.

I take a deep breath and turn the key in the lock. Pushing the weathered door open, I'm shocked to find that the inside isn't half as bad as I had expected.

It's still decorated the same as the last time I was here. The kitchen is frozen in time with its array of creams and appliances that have seen better days. I walk over to the stove, turn the knob, and am surprised to see the gas burner lights. The walls are still painted light green, now covered in a layer of dust.

I walk over to the sink to see if the water is on, hoping to get a shower in after I unpack. I twist the handle and get blasted in the face as water spews out in all directions, soaking my shirt.

"Great," I mumble to myself as I swipe the water off my face and look down at my shirt. "Oh, well. It'll dry."

I'm too overwhelmed being in this house again to worry about a damp shirt.

I continue walking, noticing the hardwood floors are scuffed with memories and discolored with age. The only furniture on the first floor seems to be the brown leather couches.

When I get upstairs, I realize the pipes in the house must be shot. The water is clearly on, but the sinks and showers are not working properly. In some cases, the water shoots out at you. In others, it trickles out.

I walk into my old bedroom and see buckets scattered about the now-empty room. Aside from the leather couches in the family room, all the furniture in the house is gone. I dreadfully lean over to peek into the buckets and see light brown water. Following the lines of gravity, I glance up and see the water damage in the ceiling as the yellow stain stares me in the face.

Crap. There's probably mold up there. I need to get a contractor in here immediately if I don't want to breathe those toxins in all summer.

I try to make a mental list of all the things that need attention. By the end, I feel the signs of a headache beginning.

I need some fresh air.

I open the sliding door that reveals the best part of the entire place—a large deck with a view of the river.

Our town sits on a small section of land right off the Skidaway River, which is a saltwater river that connects to the Atlantic Ocean.

I look out and see sailing and fishing boats pass by, and memories of my childhood come flooding back.

Dad would sit on the dock with me as we watched, trying to guess their names. It's the first real memory of him since his death that makes my heart ache. Once again, I'm that seventeen-year-old girl just looking for stability in a crazy, hectic world.

Why couldn't he see that I needed him? Why wasn't his love for me enough to continue on, even with a new wife?

I shake the thoughts away.

It doesn't matter anymore. He made his decision, and I wasn't part of it. Now, he left me a house that's going to cost me my own money to repair. Thanks for the parting gift, Father.

My stomach growls, reminding me that I haven't had anything to eat since this morning. I'm too exhausted to buy groceries. I don't even know if the fridge works.

I guess my only option is to go out. Maybe I'll head over to the local café that I used to go to all the time.

When I walk in, it's like time stood still all of these years. Nothing has changed—but in a good way. The place is well-kept and clean.

The front porch holds wrought iron tables and chairs. The building's teal color makes it feel beachy. The inside has the same teal on the walls, with dark blue booths along the perimeter and tables scattered in the middle of the room.

The place is crowded with people laughing and enjoying their meals together. I don't want to take up a table for just myself, so I walk to the bar, where there's an empty seat at the end. There's one bartender who looks like he's trying to do the work of two. I grab a menu and look over the options.

The menu looks revamped from the last time I was here. It offers fresh seafood, but the dishes are different. The flavors in the descriptions of the food make my mouth water with anticipation.

The crispy calamari is calling my name. When the bartender makes his way down to me, I give him my order and add a well-deserved glass of white wine.

It feels strange to order alcohol here. I remember many nights as a teen, desperately trying to find a place that would serve us. It never worked. The memory alone has me smiling.

The bartender places the glass in front of me. My first sip goes down smoothly and gives the much-needed relief from the day I've had.

"Oh my gosh," a familiar voice says from behind the bar. "Charlotte?"

I look up to find Layla, my best friend whom I spent every summer with when we visited. Somehow, over the years, we lost touch.

"Layla?" I exclaim.

"I can't believe it's you." She walks to my end of the bar and leans over. "What brings you here? It's been years. I never thought I'd see you here again."

A twinge of guilt stabs me in the chest.

"I know. I'm sorry it's taken so long for me to come back. I'm actually here because…" I struggle to get the words out, "my dad passed away and left me the vacation house."

Her face falls. "I'm so sorry. I hadn't heard about your dad."

I shrug my shoulders, not sure how to broach the subject with someone I've lost contact with for so long. "Thanks," I say awkwardly.

"I was surprised no one ever came back to use it. I've driven by so many times over the years. Although he did always pay someone to clean it, Mrs. Everly has done her best to keep up with it. Though I think it was only a couple of times a year he asked her to clean."

Realization strikes. "That's why it wasn't nearly as dirty as I was expecting, but it needs a lot of work. There are also some buckets in my old room catching water leaking from the ceiling."

She nods her head in understanding. "Well, how long are you staying for?"

"I was planning on staying the summer. I can work remotely during the day and plan to work on the house after hours."

"Are you fixing it up to sell it?"

I sigh. "That's the plan. My father and I didn't have the best relationship in the last decade. The house doesn't really hold memories that make me feel like hanging onto it, but it's going to be one heck of a summer trying to bring it back to the point where it's ready to sell. The water isn't working at all throughout the house. I need that fixed pronto so I can shower."

"My oldest brother Asher owns his own construction company. They do a lot of residential work. I can give you his number if you want."

My heart races a bit at the mention of her brother's name. Asher is the oldest of her three brothers, but I always had such a crush on him. I don't know what it was about him that separated him so much from his brothers.

His easy laugh and kind nature were just so alluring to me. I wonder what he's like today. He's probably married with a family.

"That would be great. Thank you so much. How've you been? You like working at the café?"

"I actually own this place. Bought it a few years back from the original owners who were looking to retire."

My jaw drops. "Layla, that's amazing! I'm so proud of you. No wonder this menu looks so incredible. I did always love whatever food you prepared for us."

It's true. She was always a phenomenal cook, even in high school. It just seemed to come naturally to her.

"Thanks." She smiles brightly. "It's been busy, but everything I dreamed of."

Just as my calamari comes out, Layla takes a look around the restaurant.

"Hey, you enjoy your food. I'm gonna do another lap to make sure everything is running smoothly. I'll come back soon."

"Absolutely. Don't worry about me. I'll be here enjoying your delicious food."

As Layla runs around the restaurant like a champ, helping where needed, I enjoy the best calamari I've ever had. She has it flavored with some kind of hot peppers, which is perfectly complimented by the tang of the lemon.

I can't believe I ran into her my first couple of hours here. Over the years, I've often thought about Layla. We were so close and had the best time together. She made my summers here what they were.

As I eat, my brain drifts back to her brother. When I was seventeen, he was twenty-two and fresh out of college. I can't remember the name of the woman he was dating, but I envied her.

She looked nothing like me. Where she had blue eyes and blonde hair, I had brown hair and hazel eyes. She was tall and skinny. I am average height with a bit of a curvy figure.

When I was at Layla's house, and nobody thought I was look-ing, I would watch how he was with her. He always had his hands on her, smiling, kissing her cheek, attending to her needs.

I vowed that summer to make sure I'd find a boyfriend just like Asher.

To say I've failed at that would be an understatement. My luck with men is almost laughable.

"Okay," Layla says as she stands back in her spot at the end of the bar. "Sorry about that."

"No problem at all."

"I still can't believe you're here, and for the entire summer. It's just like we're teenagers again. Give me your number. We have to hang out."

I reach into my purse and pull out my business card.

She looks down, and her eyes widen.

"You work for the NFL?" she gasps with excitement. "Are you freakin' kidding me?"

I giggle at her response. I'm used to it by now. I find it amusing how grown adults can still act like kids over silly things. It's refreshing to be around someone who is willing to show that side of them.

"Yes, I work for the NFL. I'm a Marketing Manager, but my cell phone number is on there."

"Oh yeah." She reaches for a pen and paper behind her. "Here's Asher's cell."

My stomach does a weird flip-flop as I watch her write down my high school crush's number for me. I can't believe my body is reacting like this after all this time.

"Give him a call. I'm sure he remembers you." Doubtful, I think to myself. "He's really good and can probably help get your water working quickly. If not, just give me a call. You are always welcome to stay at my place for a little while."

"Thanks," I smile as I take the paper from her. "That's so kind of you."

"Well, I should get back to work. It was so nice running into you."

"You too," I tell her, and I mean it.

Seeing her again feels like no time at all has passed between us. I have always felt like my true self in this town.

I think that's why it was so painful when Dad tarnished the memories for me.

On my way back to the house, my nerves go into overdrive. I need the water working as soon as possible, which means I can waste no time calling Asher.

Chapter Two

Asher

"Dude, you need to move. This house is way too small for the two of you," my brother Eric says to me.

"Noted," I grumble over the pot of chili on the stove, trying to focus on the smell of the food rather than his words.

He leans further back into the chair at the kitchen table. "I'm serious. I don't understand why you were in such a hurry to move out of the other house."

My hand grips the spatula with such force that I'm surprised it doesn't snap.

Nobody knows why I moved so quickly, and that's how I intend to keep it. But it doesn't stop the secret from tearing me up on the inside. I'm just hoping one day, I'll wake up and find that the anger inside of me is gone.

Today is not that day.

"Daddy!" my three-year-old, and the only thing that can make me smile, comes walking up to me.

I lean down to pick her up and kiss her chubby little cheek.

"Hi, Brielle. Where's Aunt Layla?"

"Auntie Layla potty," she says to me.

She's really coming along with her words. It's made it a lot easier to be able to have a small conversation with her where she can tell me what she wants. It speeds up the process rather than trying to guess why she's throwing a tantrum.

"Come here, cupcake," Eric calls to Brielle.

I put her down so she can trot over to him while I add some spices to my chili. Cooking was never something I was very good at, but ever since my wife passed away two years ago, I've made a point to learn.

I don't want my daughter to grow up eating bachelor food. I want her to thrive in this world.

Layla joins Eric at the table along with my other brother Liam.

Layla sighs. "Brie, you're cute, but you're exhausting."

"You can't keep up with a three-year-old?" Liam says with a smirk.

"Oh, please, like you could do better," Layla quips back at him.

Brie looks back and forth between my siblings, curiosity etched on her face. I know she has no idea what they're saying, but the look on her face says she's trying to figure it out, trying to decipher their words.

"Hey, Ash," Layla shouts my way. "I ran into my friend Charlotte at the café. Do you remember her? Her family would spend the summers here. In the vacant house on Bluff Drive?"

"I remember," I say with fake interest, a skill I've mastered in the last two years, so nobody bothers me with questions.

"Well, her father passed away and left the house to her. She's going to spend the summer here to work on the house and get it fixed up. She needs a contractor. I gave her your cell."

"Got it. Thanks," I reply.

Ma and Pa walk through the door, and Brie giggles with glee.

"Nana...Papa," she squeals as she wiggles out of Eric's arms to run to them.

I hear them fuss over her from the front door. If it weren't for my parents, I don't know what I would have done when Lauren passed away. They have helped raise Brie with me. I just hope it's all enough love for her since she won't have her own mother's love growing up.

When the anger starts to feel like it's going to consume me, I just think about Brie and the childhood she deserves. That helps tame the demons inside of me so I don't take it out on my innocent little girl.

"Hi, sweetie," Ma says as she kisses me on the cheek. "It smells wonderful in here."

She puts down her famous apple crisp on the counter, turns the oven on to warm it, and then puts her dish inside.

"Thanks, Ma."

I've gotten used to hosting the family over on Sundays. It used to be at my parents' place, but when Brie was younger, it was easier to put her in her crib for bed and not have to deal with transferring her at the end of the night.

My place might be a little small, but Eric is being dramatic. We all fit fine in here. This was the only house that I could find on the market in the winter, so I took it.

I needed to get out of my old home. It was suffocating. Every room was filled with memories of her, and I needed to forget. It was the only chance I had of surviving, of letting the truth swallow me whole.

"You guys made it just in time. Chili is ready," I shout. "Everybody grab a bowl."

"You aren't serving us?" Eric asks from the table.

"I'm not your frickin' servant. Get your lazy butt out of my chair, that's probably also too small for you, and come get your dinner."

After everyone has their food, we all take our seats around my table. Brie insists she sits on Liam's lap, but he doesn't seem to mind as he begins to eat over her head.

"This chili is hot, man," I say to him. "Try not to drop it on my daughter's head."

He eyes me with annoyance. "I wouldn't hurt my niece. Maybe you should try to chill out and even smile once in a while."

I brace for everyone to chime in with their opinions. Telling me I'm different since Lauren passed, that I should get help, that I don't smile anymore. Telling me I'm angry at the world and should find things to be happy about or asking me what else happened that hardened me to life.

"Daddy, this yummy," Brie chimes in.

I wink at her, and she giggles. She doesn't actually understand that she saved me on that one, but I appreciate it.

Layla starts talking to our parents about her friend who's back in town, and my mind begins to wander. I remember Charlotte. Most of the time, she was just my sister's friend, but the last summer I saw her, she really started to mature. I tried not to take notice since she was seventeen, but it was impossible not to.

However, I was too enamored with Lauren to care, and Charlotte was far too young for me at the time. She was still in high school when I had already finished college.

I remember spotting her on the dock with her father all the time. I would smile every time my boat went passed and I saw her.

I've driven by that house a number of times over the years. I don't know what the inside looks like, but if the outside is any indication, Charlotte has her work cut out for her this summer.

If I gave a shit about anything anymore, I would be a little worried about her spending nights alone in that place until it was inspected. But that man died a long time ago.

My family has all but begged me to see a therapist. They think someone can talk me out of this *funk*, but they don't know the full story. No one does.

That's how it will stay—for my daughter's sake.

Just as I'm finishing my chili, my phone buzzes in my pocket. An area code I don't recognize flashes across the screen. Most of the time, unknown numbers are work calls, but running a company means taking calls twenty-four/seven.

"Excuse me," I announce to the table. "Hello, this is Asher."

"Hi, Asher. My name is Charlotte. I'm an old friend of Layla's," Charlotte says softly on the phone.

I get an odd feeling in my chest at the sound of her voice. I wonder if I'm getting heartburn from that chili. Am I too young for heartburn?

"Yes, my sister told me you'd be calling," I reply.

"Oh, um, okay. Well, I'm not sure what exactly she told you."

I step out onto the small patio in my backyard to take the call, wanting some privacy from the many ears in my kitchen.

"Just said you needed some renovations done on your house."

"Well, the thing is," she begins hesitantly. "The water isn't working. In some sinks, it splashes out all over, and in others, it just trickles out. I normally wouldn't have called at this hour, but I just wanted to see if this is something your company can handle or if I should be calling a plumber."

I squeeze the back of my neck as tension grows. We normally don't get to a house quickly for emergency repairs. We're more of a home renovation kind of company, but she sounds so desperate on the phone.

I think I might feel bad for her. Shit, maybe there's a heart somewhere inside me. Or maybe I just want to avoid the wrath of Layla if I pass her friend off to someone else when she's clearly desperate.

"I can take a look. I normally have my guys go out on the repairs, but I don't make them work weekends. I have some time tomorrow afternoon to come take a look."

I hear a sigh of relief on the phone. "Oh, thank you so much. Do you need my address? I can text it to this number."

"I know the house. I'll text you when I'm getting ready to head your way."

"That's great. I really appreciate you fitting me in last minute."

"It's fine. I'll see you tomorrow."

"Oh, uh, sure. Thanks again. Bye."

I end the call and curse under my breath. I know how I come off these days. I wish I knew how to control it, but I don't have it in me to try and figure it out. I'm just...tired.

I'm tired of living my life with this lie. Tired that life can be so cruel. Tired that people can go on living like they're innocent when the world deserves to know their cruelty.

I walk back inside and take a seat. Everybody is still laughing and talking while Brielle has now moved to my dad's lap.

"Who was that?" Ma asks.

"Layla's friend, Charlotte. I have to head over there tomorrow to take a look at the plumbing. She's at their old family home, and the water is shot. Any chance I could drop off Brie around one before I go there?"

Ma smiles at me. "Of course. I was going to bake a peach cobbler. I have some lovely Georgia peaches that I picked up from the farm the other day. Speaking of, let me go get the apple crisp."

I look over at Layla and notice her giving me the death stare.

"What?" I say as I roll my eyes.

"You better be nice to her. She just lost her dad, and she's been through a lot. I can tell."

"I don't think what I say or don't say to her will make much of a difference. I'm going over there to fix her plumbing."

"There's a sexual innuendo in there somewhere. I just can't think of a good one," Liam says, clearly not really paying attention to the conversation.

Layla rolls her eyes. "You're thinking too hard. Don't hurt your-self."

"You guys have fun acting like teenagers. I'm going to go put Brie to bed." I stand up and grab my daughter, who is now rubbing her eyes.

She rests her head on my chest, and I feel my heart turn to mush. I love these moments. They make me feel like there's still a decent man inside.

Chapter Three

Charlotte

I stare down at the contents of items I purchased this morning that are now scattered all over the kitchen island:

cleaning products, tools, gallons of water so I can brush my teeth and stay hydrated until I figure out this plumbing issue. I almost took Layla up on her offer last night to shower at her place, but I didn't know what time she got off work and didn't have it in me to bug her the very night we reconnected. It just felt wrong.

As I try to shuffle through all the items that I bought, my thoughts drift back to my conversation with Asher last night. I don't know what I was expecting the man on the other line to be like, but what I got wasn't it.

He was kind of short with me and his voice sounded distant and uninterested. I'm shocked he agreed to come take a look today.

I'm probably just being stupid about it. Just because I had a little crush on him ten years ago doesn't mean we were going to have some profound conversation. He's probably married and was distracted while talking to me, and here I am, analyzing our conversation.

"Ugh, get a grip, Charlotte," I scold myself.

I just need to focus on the task at hand, which is power washing the outside of the house. I bought some fancy-looking power washer that should help me remove all the chipped paint off the deck.

I want to sand and stain the deck once I'm finished. It seems like a good task for me to focus on for a little while. How hard can it be?

First things first, I want to deep clean the house. It's definitely not horrible, but it needs a good scrubbing on every surface to bring it back to present day.

I pour two gallons of water into a bucket and mix it with the cleaner. My goal is to first take the sponges to the baseboards and walls. I grab my portable speaker and blast Taylor Swift as I begin in the kitchen.

After I scrub the baseboards on the first floor, I start to scrub the inside and outside of the kitchen cabinets. Now that I know the appliances work, I want to get some groceries today.

My arm is already protesting my cleaning, but I do my best to ignore it. Good thing I picked up some coffee this morning. I'm going to need it with the work I have cut out for me today.

I climb onto the counters, finish the upper cabinets, and move to the bottom. Thankfully, I can do these while sitting down—I'm not afraid to admit I'm lazy and will take a seat whenever possible. I'm also thankful that the HVAC is still working. I'd be dying in an inferno right now if it wasn't.

Just as I finish the last cabinet, there's a knock at the door.

"Shit," I whisper as I look down at myself.

I don't know what time it is, but I must've missed Asher's text. Somewhere in the middle of all the cleaning, I ditched my sweaty t-shirt.

Now, I'm in just my shorts and a sports bra. When a second knock comes, I throw the sponge in the bucket and run to the door.

I open it to find Asher looking down at his phone.

He's in light jeans, work boots, a white t-shirt that fits his clearly defined body like a damn glove, and sunglasses.

If I thought twenty-two-year-old Asher was good-looking, he was nothing compared to thirty-two-year-old Asher. This man is all muscle—tan, broody, perfectly sculpted face with such defined features. It actually takes my breath away.

But when he looks up at me, his mouth turns down as if he isn't happy with what he sees. It kind of makes my entire body deflate with disappointment.

"Hi. I'm so sorry. I've been busy cleaning. I didn't hear my phone go off," I say as I run a hand through the loose hair that has fallen from my ponytail.

I must look like a complete mess. Maybe he's grossed out.

"It's fine," is all he says as he steps inside the house. "I'll just go ahead and look around."

"Um, okay," I whisper to myself as I shut the door, but he's already gone.

My initial impression of him on the phone last night seems to be spot on. Asher Williams has turned into a *dick*.

I didn't even invite him in. He all but pushed me aside to get in and get to work. Not even a *how are you* or *how have you been since the last time I saw you ten years ago?*

I walk back to the kitchen to grab my bucket just as he's coming up from the basement. I presume to shut the water off like a smart person would do before they take a look at the plumbing.

Instead of saying anything to me or offering a smile, he looks me up and down and then grunts to himself.

Seriously, what the hell happened to this man? This is not the Asher I once knew and pined over secretly for years.

Well, I don't know how long it's going to take him so I might as well get back to work. I was initially planning on showing him around and watching him inspect in case he had any questions for me. But he clearly is not interested in my company.

So, I grab my bucket and bring it to the foyer to start to work on cleaning the walls. I turn my stereo back on and do my best to tune out the gorgeous yet rude man upstairs.

The walls have so much filth on them that I'm shocked to see how much cleaner they look with just a glide of the sponge. I still think they could use a coat of fresh paint, as can the baseboards, but this is a good start to breathing in some fresh air.

I don't know how long I get lost in the music as I scrub my little heart away. At some point, when I'm shaking my behind to Shake It Off, I hear a loud throat clearing behind me, which makes me throw my sponge in the air and jump.

"Oh my gosh!" I shout over the music as my hand flies to my heart. "You scared me. I forgot you were here."

It's been over an hour. I finished the foyer and just about done with the family room. I'm almost done with the entire first floor, actually.

"I think I know what's going on," he starts, ignoring the fact that he scared me half to death. "I also did an inspection of different areas I saw that needed work. Do you want to sit down outside and go over everything?"

"Um, sure. The back deck is the only place with seating anyway. We can go out there," I tell him as I return the sponge back to the bucket and lead him outside.

We walk in awkward silence the entire way to the deck. I take a seat across from him and watch as he pulls out his notepad.

I'm still waiting for him to show any signs of recognition or interest in my life since I've been gone, but it seems southern hospitality doesn't apply anymore where Asher Williams is concerned.

Instead, he gets straight to business.

"So, let's start with the plumbing. I had to take apart some of the pipes, but I did find corrosion inside the parts that I dismantled. The discoloration of the outside of the pipes is enough for me to say that all of the pipes need to be replaced."

I'm sure he can see the look of horror on my face. I need to shower and use the bathroom. Although the toilets have flushed so far, I'm just waiting for them to give out on me.

"How long does that take?" I ask.

He scratches the back of his head. "Well, I could get it done in two days with the help of a buddy of mine. Since we aren't talking about commercial pipes, we could get them from our distributor immediately."

"And the cost?"

"We're looking at about three grand for the pipes."

That's not a small chunk of change, but I was expecting worse. My blood pressure begins to come down a bit.

I can handle that. Three grand and two days.

"When can you start?"

"I need to call my buddy to see when he's free, but I think we could start tomorrow. It's Sunday, so I wasn't supposed to work, which means I have nothing on the schedule. Monday, I can move some things around."

I sigh with relief. "Oh my gosh! Thank you so much. I really appreciate you doing this for me."

He looks at me like the words I said are offensive. "I'm not doing anything for *you*. I'm doing my job."

"Oh, right. Sorry, I wasn't implying anything. I...just...appreciate it."

He nods his head.

"Moving on," he says as he looks back down at his notes. I try to focus on his words, but I'm too stunned at the cruel, bitter man sitting in front of me. "There is definitely some mold in the room upstairs with the leaks. Since we have to rip out drywall to replace pipes, we can take care of that, no problem."

"I didn't even think about that. Will you be repairing the drywall after?"

"We can. It will be another five hundred, but that will extend the project by another couple of days. I will send in my drywall crew afterward to get that fixed up." I nod my head, trying to remain polite and upbeat despite his overall demeanor. "Aside from that, it does just seem like maybe some wear and tear that needs to be updated, but nothing too bad. I'd say you could sneak by with the roof for another couple of years."

"I do want to repaint the outside of the house, and I would like to refinish the hardwood floors."

"Those are easy. We could do those in a matter of a couple of weeks. I could work up a quote for you on the rest and email it to you this week."

"That would be great."

He pulls out a piece of paper. "Just fill this out so I have your contact information. I generally just need your email so I can make sure to get you the quote."

He begins to stand up and continues, "Other than that, I will be in touch, but I do believe I will be out here first thing in the morning to start on the pipes."

"Sounds good. Thanks again," I say while handing him my information back, and he walks off the stairs of the back deck.

"It's my job," he reiterates. "I'll see you tomorrow."

With that, he disappears around the house. I sit back down on my chair and look out at the lake.

Gosh, I remember seeing his parents' boat go by on the water and wishing I could catch a glimpse of him without a shirt on.

I was young and hormones were raging.

Something must've happened. You don't turn that ice cold in life for no reason. I wonder what it could've been.

Chapter Four

Asher

"Fucking asshole," I mutter to myself as I drive away from her house.

I know I was a dick. I'm usually guarded and quiet but not so obviously rude. I wasn't expecting her to open the door wearing next to nothing and looking so damn good.

Why does that piss me off so much?

It shouldn't. I see plenty of beautiful women all the time. Most of them practically throw themselves at me at the bar or at Layla's café.

This is different. I don't know what it is, but I felt my heart beat faster, and my body started to react. I haven't had a reaction like that to a woman since I met Lauren. It was like my entire body came to life, and everything else around me faded away.

But I try not to think about Lauren. It's been two years since she passed away from cancer, and just the thought of her can send me into a tailspin.

Why does seeing Charlotte elicit such a reaction, though? I don't know, but I sure as hell hope it was just a fluke.

Maybe I just need to rub one out tonight, and I'll be less tense tomorrow. I don't remember how long it's been since I've even done that.

After I pick Brie up from my parents' house, we settle in at home for dinner. I make her favorite mac and cheese with a side of steamed broccoli.

Brie actually likes her vegetables, but I've made a point of having them out for every meal since she was old enough to eat solid foods. If I notice that she eats more of a certain type, I will cook that more often.

"Yummy. Mac n cheese," she squeals with a big smile as she tries to scoop an overflowing spoonful of noodles onto her fork.

I smile as I watch her struggle.

"Did you have fun with Nana and Papa today?"

She nods her head, which makes her noodles fall off her fork. Giving up on it, she grabs a handful and shovels it into her mouth. Whatever floats her boat. She's getting a bath after dinner anyway, and I'm in no rush to force her to grow up quickly.

"What did you do with them?" I ask, then take a bite of my food.

I'm not gonna lie, an excuse to eat this food at my age is kinda nice. I don't think you can ever outgrow your love for mac and cheese.

"Play blocks. Papa push them," she explains then tries to show me with her hands.

She loves it when someone builds blocks with her and then destroys them together. She cracks up after they all fall to the ground.

After we finish our dinner together, I give her a bath, and we snuggle down to watch an episode of her favorite cartoon. I don't always have the energy to play with her all the way until bedtime, but these moments when I can still snuggle with her while letting my body and brain rest are nice to have.

Once I notice her eyes begin to look heavy, I take that as my sign to get her into bed. I rock her and sing her two songs, which is our normal routine, and then I put her in her bed.

I tiptoe out even though she isn't sleeping yet. It's a habit from when she was an infant that I haven't broken yet. There was nothing worse than thinking she was fast asleep just to step on a creaky floorboard and hear the crying start again.

As soon as I fall back on the couch, I close my eyes and take a moment to myself.

Being a single parent is exhausting. There's never time to myself. The only time I get is once Brie is in bed for the night, and by then, I'm so damn tired that I'm ready to crash myself.

My phone buzzes in my jeans. When I pull it out, I see a text from my buddy Josh telling me he can make it tomorrow, which is a relief. There was no way I was getting those pipes installed in two days without his help.

The muscles in my body are tense. I normally use the weekend to recover from the grueling strain on them during the week. I make a point to never work on the weekends.

But I didn't want her going longer than necessary without water. What I should be doing is assigning two of my guys to start on her house on Monday. It's what I would've done with any other job.

I'm not sure what made me personally take the job on. It can't just be because I'm attracted to her, even though my brain floods with images of her small waist and yet round ass and generous breasts.

My dick twitches in my jeans at just one image of her body.

Shit. I'm so screwed.

After dropping Brie off at my parents, I drove my truck to my distributor and picked up the pipes I needed for Charlotte's house.

Now, I'm on my way to her house with all the supplies.

The more I thought about my interaction with her yesterday, the more I realized how unfair I was to her. I'm sure it was a one-time thing just thrown off by her beauty, but I still owe an apology. She didn't deserve it.

When I pull into her drive, Josh is already there leaning against his struck with a thermos of coffee in his hand.

He nods at me as my feet crunch along the gravel. "Morning, man."

I shake my head. "I should've known you'd be early."

"On time is late in this business," he says with a smile.

"Thanks for doing this on such late notice and for giving up your Sunday."

He shrugs. "Work is work."

We walk up to the front door, but before I can knock, it swings open.

Charlotte is in another sports bra and shorts get up. My jaw clenches in instant anger. What the hell is with this woman and not wearing clothes?

She wipes her forehead with the back of her hand. "Hi. I'm so sorry. I keep losing track of time. I've been scrubbing this place from top to bottom for two days now."

Josh smiles at her. "You do know that we're about to tear it up. Right?"

Charlotte lets out a soft laugh. "I know. I still needed to do it for my own sanity."

Watching the two of them smile and laugh with each other stirs something inside of me. I want to tell him to back the fuck off, but she's not mine. It's best to remember that I don't date anymore.

I don't care what my damn body feels toward Charlotte. Dating went out the window ever since the night my world came crashing down.

But when I see Josh look her body up and down, I've never wanted my fist to meet his face more.

"Come on in," she says directly to Josh. Her eyes meet mine with hesitancy. "Hi, Asher."

"Hi," I say to her without meeting her eyes. It feels too intimate, too dangerous to look directly in those beautiful green eyes while I talk.

My apology has gone out the window. All I feel right now is pure adrenaline coursing through me. Since I can't take it out on her in the way I believe my body would like to, it appears my only other option is through rage.

Josh turns to me in the foyer. "Are we gonna start in the basement and work our way up?"

I nod at him in agreement. "We'll be downstairs. I'm going to have to shut the water off, so nothing will be functioning for a couple hours."

"Got it. I'll refrain from all bathroom use until further notice."

I do my best to not look directly at the sweat dripping down her cleavage, but it's not the easiest thing to do. When I move up to her face, her green eyes are just as mesmerizing. Dammit, I don't know where to look.

I turn around and hustle downstairs like distance is gonna save me from these feelings. As soon as I'm downstairs, I take a much-needed deep breath.

When I look over at Josh, I notice him eyeing me with a smirk.

"What?" I ask in annoyance.

He shrugs. "Nothing. She's pretty, isn't she?"

"I don't know. I didn't notice," I reply.

I put down my tools and began inspecting the pipes above me as if I had not just uttered the most ridiculously obvious lie.

Josh chuckles as he sets down his own set of tools. "You didn't notice, eh?"

"Nope." I'm short with him. "Okay, you ready to start bringing in the pipes?"

He gives me a knowing smile that I choose to ignore. Josh is one of my buddies that I've grown up with. He was around when Lauren passed and has been trying like hell to get me out in the dating scene again.

I've told him hundreds of times that I'm not interested in a relationship ever again, but he seems to think I'll come around.

After we get the pipes that we need to replace downstairs, we begin to work together to take the old ones out.

"You missed an interesting night out last night," he tells me.

"Did I?"

"Kyle invited Avery and Layla."

"I still can't believe Kyle and Avery are together," I say as I work on connecting the new pipes.

Kyle is another buddy we grew up with, and Avery is friends with my sister Layla.

"Yeah. It's weird to have her around all the time. And you need to talk to your sister, man," he grumbles in frustration. "She flirts with every guy that looks at her."

I sigh. "I'm not trying that again. Last time I did, she nearly bit my head off for 'cock-blocking' her. I don't need my sister talking to me about cocks, so I vowed to stay the hell out of it."

"She's a piece of work."

I smile as I listen to him vent about my sister.

After we get all the pipes replaced in the basement within a couple of hours, we take a seat to catch our breaths. The more difficult part of this process will be the first and second floors, where we have to cut holes in the drywall to change the pipes. We lucked out that the basement wasn't finished.

"You wanna go grab some lunch before we start on the next floor?" Josh asks as he lifts his hat and wipes the sweat off his forehead.

"Definitely. Where do you wanna go? The café?" I ask.

I see him stiffen at the suggestion, then try to cover it up. He gets weird every time I suggest the place. If I didn't know any better, I'd say there's something going on between him and my sister. That, or he just hates the food and doesn't want to say it.

I think about my sister's food for a second. Nah, there's no way he hates the food. Her food is better than any expensive restaurant I've ever eaten at.

"Aren't we meeting up with the guys there for dinner tonight?" he points out.

Damn. He's right. They like to meet up at least once a month. I try to get out of it, even managed to successfully for a year after Lauren passed, before Josh started forcing me to go again.

"I forgot. You just wanna grab something fast?"

"Yeah. Let's go. I'm gonna die of a heat stroke if we don't get some food and water in me soon."

We walk up the stairs and out the front door but are blasted with a loud sound coming from the front porch. As I descend down the stairs, I see Charlotte using a machine sander as she moves it around the railings of the porch.

The woman is covered head to toe in sawdust. When she notices us standing there, she switches the sander off and turns toward us with a smile on her face.

"What's up?" she says cheerfully.

"What in the hell are you doing?" I blurt out as I look at the mess.

That's not exactly how I meant it to sound, but she isn't wearing a mask and is probably inhaling so many dangerous chemicals right now.

"Um, I'm sanding the wood so I can stain it."

"You do know there's a piece of equipment that goes to that sander to collect the dust so it doesn't fly all over you, right?" Josh says to her.

She rips off her sunglasses and drops her shoulders. "Are you serious?"

Josh chuckles. "Take a look in that box. I'm sure it's in there."

He points to the box that was holding the sander. She obviously just purchased it and has no clue what the hell she is doing.

She peeks inside and pulls out the small cloth pieces that twists onto the sanding device. "This thing?" she questions as she holds it up.

For the first time in forever, I feel a smile, wanting to break free at how damn cute and innocent she looks right now.

"That would be the one," Josh says. He steps toward her and grabs it from her hand.

As he twists it onto the sander for her, I take the opportunity to look at her. She certainly isn't like any woman I've ever met. Clearly, she's willing to get sweaty and do some manual labor.

It adds a whole other element to her attractiveness, other than her incredible curves. When my eyes look from her ass all the way up her body, I'm met with her eyes looking right back at me.

I don't know what to do since I was just caught checking her out. I quickly look away like that somehow will make it better.

When I look back at her, there's a small look of amusement across her face. Yeah, she knows exactly what I was doing. I feel like a complete idiot.

"So, any chance at least one of the showers is gonna be ready today?" she asks me as she glances down at her body. "I'm clearly gonna need one."

"I think we could run the pipes up one side of the house into the master. I'll have to tape some plastic over the area of the shower that gets cut out to access the pipes."

The look of relief on her face is evident. "Oh my gosh! Seriously? That would be amazing."

"Well, you could definitely use a shower," I reply.

The small smile on her face fades. Shit, that wasn't the right thing to say.

I didn't mean it like that. For once, I tried to be polite, and it still came out like an insult. It's like I don't even know how to be nice anymore.

I think I was going for funny, lighthearted, since she's covered in dust. Somehow, that came out like I was telling her she smells like a barnyard animal and needs soap and water immediately.

Josh chuckles. "Don't mind my friend here. He comes off as scary, but he's harmless. We're heading out for lunch. Can we bring you back anything?"

"Oh, wow. That would be great. Thank you so much," she smiles at him, then turns to me, and her smile fades.

It pisses me off more than it should. Why does he get those reactions from her? More importantly, why do I want those from her? I shouldn't.

Josh hops in my truck, but before I'm even out of the driveway, he's on my ass.

"Dude, what the fuck is your problem?" he asks accusingly. "Are you trying to be a dick to her?"

I run my hand through my hair in frustration. "Of course, I'm not trying. I meant it as a joke. If you said it, she would've laughed."

"Yeah, well, if I said it, I would've had a damn smile on my face. You can't have a scowl on your face and tell somebody how badly they need a shower."

I hate it when he's right. There used to be a time when I was that happy-go-lucky, carefree kinda guy. That feels like ages ago.

"Wait a minute," Josh says. "You were trying to make a joke? Since when do you joke around with anyone anymore, Mr. Grumpypants?"

My body tenses at the realization that he's on to me. Deny, deny, deny. That's my plan.

"I joke around plenty of times," I lie.

He throws his head back in laughter. "That's the biggest load of shit I've heard all year. Between your reaction to her when we walked up to the house and you trying to joke around with her...I'm thinking someone *likes* her."

"I don't know what you're talking about. I don't like her. She's my client. I was trying to ease her worries."

"Alright, so you're not ready to admit it. That's fine. Or I'm wrong, and I can go for her. She was pretty adorable, covered in sawdust, trying to do that project on her own."

I know he's trying to get a rise out of me, and it's not going to work. I clench my jaw to refrain from saying anything incriminating.

Even if I do like her, I would never do anything about it. I won't put myself out there like that again.

Chapter Five

Charlotte

Sanding a porch sucks. This is the work of the devil. Every muscle in my body is screaming at me to stop. Who the hell knew it would take so much stamina to get this shit off?

I sure as hell didn't. I thought the sander was going to do all the work for me, but the strength it takes to push down and keep it in place is brutal.

But I'm too damn proud and stubborn to admit to myself or Asher that I'm in over my head.

The front door swings open, and the guys walk out laughing about something. I take the chance to look at Josh's unrestrained laugh compared to Asher's careful and controlled one.

The two men are so different. Josh is good-looking, too, but he's also easy-going and kind—the way Asher used to be.

When Asher approaches, I turn off the sander, bracing myself for another insult, like how badly my breath smells.

Honestly, it probably does. They've had the water off all day, minus the hour they were gone for lunch.

"The master shower is working, and the water is turned back on," Asher says as he leans against the railing.

"That is such a relief." My shoulders sag at the thought of relaxing under a stream of steaming hot water.

His eyes look between me and the sander with slight amusement. "You know, I could get the porch and back deck done for you. It would save you a lot of time."

My eyebrows scrunch together in annoyance. "I'm aware I could pay you to do it, but seeing as my father only left me this place and not a dime to go with it, I can't afford for you to do everything."

I think I see a faint glint of guilt in his eyes. "I'm sorry. I didn't mean it like that. I was just letting you know my company could provide the service if you needed."

Crap, now I feel bad.

"I'm sorry. I didn't mean for my words to come out so harsh."

He looks bewildered by my quick apology. Clearly, not something he does so easily to someone.

"No problem. Anyway, I'll be back out here tomorrow to finish the work. Josh has to be back at his current job site tomorrow. I'll be here bright and early so I can try to knock out the rest of the project tomorrow."

It's so hard to figure him out. His actions say he's a decent man who runs a good company and offers to help a relative stranger out when they're in a bind, even if it means him giving up his weekend. But his words and demeanor say something entirely different.

When he opens his mouth, his actions are overshadowed by the sting of his ire.

"I appreciate it. I'll see you tomorrow," I tell him.

Josh smiles at me. "It was nice to meet you, Charlotte."

"You too, Josh. Thanks for helping out on such short notice."

"My pleasure. I hope I'll see you around this summer."

He winks and solutes Asher, who is currently giving him a death stare, which only seems to make Josh laugh as he walks away.

"Bye, Charlotte," Asher says in his deep timbered voice.

He walks away, and I turn the sander back on. I hate how there's still a part of me that's so attracted to him. Get a grip, Charlotte.

I begin to mindlessly sand the same spot while my eyes remain glued to Asher. He opens his truck door but doesn't hop in right away. Instead, I watch him reach in his front seat for something, but I can't see what it is.

His hand grabs the back of his shirt, and the next thing I know, I'm staring at his bare back.

I audibly gasp. Thankfully, I have this sander on, so no one can hear me losing my shit over here.

Every damn muscle in his back is thick and toned. My jaw is on the floor, but I can't seem to pick it up.

He grabs what seems to be a clean white t-shirt off his seat, giving me a view of the front of his body. The lines and grooves in his abs are hotter than anything I've ever seen.

He starts to turn back toward his truck, so I lean forward to try and catch the last glimpse of his chest, forgetting I have the powerful vibrating sander on. I go flying forward as the machine takes me with it.

I let out a loud scream as I land on my stomach. The machine falls out of my hands and starts jumping around on the deck.

Before my brain can process what just happened, Asher is running up the deck. He pulls the cord, and the sander slowly comes to a stop.

My head falls forward on my arms as I shake my head. This is not happening. I did not just make a total ass of myself in front of this man.

When I pick my head back up, he's standing there with his arms crossed. He didn't even have time to put his clean shirt on, now giving me a close-up of his perfectly sculpted body.

"What happened now?" his gravelly voice asks eagerly.

"I got distracted," I say as I push off the wood and stand up, trying desperately not to stare at his abs.

I make an attempt to wipe the dust off my body, but it's futile. I'm covered head to toe and must look pitiful.

His eyebrow raises with curiosity. "What distracted you?"

"I thought I saw a bear," I lie.

Are there even bears here?

I swear I see the beginning of a smirk on his face, but he catches himself. "There aren't any bears around here."

"Yeah, well, that's why I was so shocked."

Why the hell did I say bear? We're by the ocean, not the damn mountains. This man has me out of sorts, but in my defense, it should be illegal to take your shirt off when you look as good as he does.

"That would be a shocking sight to see out here with no woods surrounding us," he says in smug delight.

Ugh, his stupid face says it all. He knows I was distracted by something else, and I'm sure he is cocky enough to suspect it's him.

"Anyway, I'm all good. Thanks for coming over to check on me."

I go to reach for the sander, but he stops me.

"Look, I really would feel a lot better if you let me at least *help* you with this project."

"I can handle it. Just because I didn't know about that stupid dust bag thing and lost control of it for a second doesn't mean I'm not capable."

He throws his hands up in defense, but all that does is give me the perfect view of his body. My damn eyes give me away as they assess the sharp lines of his abs.

"I'm just saying I would like to help—free of charge. I'm fully aware that you are capable of doing this project despite losing control of the big bad bear you thought you saw."

He winks at me. It feels playful and light. I didn't know he had it in him, but fuck, it makes my lady parts clench to see a glimpse of a lighter side.

"Ugh, just say it already. I wasn't distracted by a bear. It was you. You and your stupid…" I wave my arms in the air to gesture at his body, "muscles."

His hands come up in defense. "Hey, I never said I didn't believe you."

"Oh, please. You're about as subtle as a sledgehammer with your smirks and winks."

He bites his bottom lip to try and hide his obvious smirk. I'm not sure I like my discomfort as the reason this man suddenly can't hold back a smile.

"Come on. Just take my help," he says, ignoring my previous comment.

"I told you. I can't afford it."

"It's free of charge. I'll help you next weekend."

I eye him skeptically. "Why would you do something like that for me?"

He shrugs his shoulders. "Beats the hell out of me. I suppose I don't want your blood on my hands if something ends up happening."

"Gee, how sweet of you."

I cross my arms over my chest. His eyes immediately follow a path down to my breasts. A muscle flicks angrily in his jaw.

"Just promise me one thing," he says when his eyes meet mine again. "Wear more clothes when we work together. You're not the only one who can get distracted around here."

Did he just admit he's distracted by seeing me in my shorts and sports bra? Does he like what he sees?

I shouldn't like the feeling that evokes in me. I'm too startled by his words to offer any response.

He doesn't give me a chance to accept his offer, he just walks off the porch and hops into his truck.

Having lost the ability to think clearly, I stand in place and watch him drive off.

I don't know how we went from scowls and cruel words to admitting attraction to one another. At least, I think that's what we both just did—in a backward sort of way.

And I think I just agreed to let him help me with the front porch and deck repair. I look around at what I have left. I haven't even started the back deck, which is huge. It's probably a good idea to get his help.

My body is already killing me. I don't know how much more of this I can take.

My stomach begins to growl. It's not used to expending so much energy and needs some food to refuel. I think I'll go back to the café tonight. Maybe Layla will be there again.

I can thank her for recommending her brother and maybe also ask what the hell happened to him.

But first, I need a shower.

The place is busier than I had anticipated it to be for a Sunday night.

I take a seat at the bar, finding a single chair available at the end again. A different bartender is working tonight. He hands me a menu and tells me he'll get my drink order in a second.

I begin to survey the menu when I hear a table to my right erupt with laughter. When I look over, I see Josh laughing at something another man just said. The table has five guys at it, Asher being one of them.

All the other men are cracking up while Asher has his signature restrained smile on his face.

His blue eyes meet mine from across the room. I expect to see them darken with contempt, but to my surprise, they appear to soften. And yet, he doesn't acknowledge me.

"You're back!" Layla materializes in front of me with a huge smile on her face. "Yay!"

Her slender arms engulf me in a warm hug.

"I'm back." I laugh. "Aside from the awesome food here, I have no water to cook with."

"Oh my gosh. Did you call my brother? He's right over there if you need me to grab him."

"I actually called him the night you gave me his number. I took my first shower tonight since I've been here, thanks to him. I just don't have running water in the kitchen yet."

She claps her hands together. "Oh, good. I'm so glad that worked out. Well, what are you doing sitting here by yourself? Come over here and join the guys."

Before she can give me the time to find an excuse, she grabs me by the hand and pulls me with her. Asher's eyes are on us the entire time we walk in their direction.

"Hey, guys," Layla says as she stops in front of their table. "This is my friend Charlotte. We spent our summers together here since we were young. She will be spending the summer here again while she fixes up her dad's house."

"Charlotte. Nice to see you again," Josh says enthusiastically.

Layla turns sour. "You know her already? Figures you wouldn't miss a chance to meet a new woman in town," she snaps back at Josh.

His eyes grow smaller as he looks at her, his forehead creasing. "Yes, Layla. I worked on her house today with Asher."

I sense some serious animosity between the two.

Layla turns her attention to the rest of the guys. "Anyway, I don't want her sitting alone at the bar another night. Care to keep her company?"

Wow. Way to make me sound like a total loser, Layla. I know she didn't mean it, but yikes. I feel like a charity case right now.

"Take a seat, Charlotte," a man with dark blonde hair and piercing blue eyes gestures to the chair next to him.

I hesitantly take the seat, not sure exactly how to tell them I'm too mortified to join.

"I'm Paul," the man next to me says, "and that's Kyle and David."

"Hi, nice to meet you guys," I say to the rest of the guys.

"That's Asher," Paul adds as if he forgot.

Asher looks less than amused. "We know each other."

"We're a little short-staffed tonight, so I'm gonna be your server," Layla says with a smile. "Charlotte, what can I get you to drink?"

Layla goes down the line, taking our orders.

When she runs off to get our drinks, the guys turn their attention to me. It's a bit unnerving, but nothing is more unnerving than when my eyes meet Asher's.

His eyes rake over me, making my body burn with his perusal. I feel my nipples harden at his attention. I try not to act bothered by it, but I can tell the second he notices what his attention does to me by the small tip of his lips.

His hot and cold behavior is giving me whiplash.

"How was the shower?" Josh smiles at me. "Was it everything you were hoping for?"

I can't help but laugh. He has this lightness about him that makes him easy to be around. "It was absolutely the best shower I've ever had. Even though I was looking at how badly that bathroom needs a full update."

"Nothing your boy Ash here can't do for you. You could help her with her shower troubles, right man?" Josh winks.

I eye Asher. "Speaking of showers, am I clean enough for you now? I don't smell too bad for you to hang around?" I joke.

He studies me, scratching his chin, then leans in. "I don't know. Is there a bear around for you to get distracted by, or should I take my shirt off?"

"Woah, I feel like I've missed something," Josh cuts in as he looks between us.

Asher lifts his eyebrow, daring me to admit what happened only hours earlier.

Thankfully, Layla interrupts as she passes out our drinks. The entire time she moves around the table, Asher's eyes bore into mine. I can't get a read on him, and it's starting to piss me off.

Layla takes our food order and is gone again. I wish she could sit with us, but at least I get to be around her. It's nice having her company, even if only for a moment.

"Charlotte," Paul says as he puts his arm around my chair. The gesture makes me a bit uncomfortable, but I try to shake it off. "Where are you from?"

As I begin to answer Paul's questions, I notice Asher has become stiff as he watches us. His hand is gripping his beer glass so hard that I worry it'll shatter.

And that's how he remains for the rest of the evening, tight-lipped and short.

I don't know what the change was, but something made him shut down.

It stayed on my mind for the remainder of the evening, as I drove home and even as I lay awake in bed.

The way he went from cool and casual to completely expressionless and rigid doesn't seem right. I'm dying to figure him out, figure out what happened to the man I once knew.

At the end of the night, Layla and I promised to get together for lunch this week. She's going to come over and check out the house.

Maybe I should ask her about it. I'm sure she'll have some insight for me, if she's willing to share.

For now, I need to set it aside because there's no way in hell I'm bringing it up to him directly.

Chapter Six

Asher

"Please be wearing clothes today. Please be wearing clothes today," I whisper to myself after I knock on her door.

I hold my breath as the door swings open.

Shit. She's wearing clothes today. Wait, no, that's good. That's what I wanted, right?

Her long brown hair is up in a ponytail, making her look effortlessly beautiful. She's in a white sundress with a lemon print. She still looks beautiful.

A small, hesitant smile forms on her face.

"Good morning. Come on in," she says as she holds the door open for me.

I walk in, and as I pass her, I get a hint of her perfume. It's floral yet sophisticated. I feel my jeans grow tighter as the scent takes effect on me.

Easy there, boy. This one is not for you.

It appears that my body still doesn't understand that we aren't touching this one. If I got one taste, it would never be enough.

"Mornin'," I reply. "You're not dressed to work on the deck. I'll take that as an official acceptance of my offer to help."

She closes the door and follows me inside.

"Well, I have to work this week. But I wouldn't exactly call what you said an offer. It felt more like a demand."

If only I could show her what a demanding Asher looked like. I'd tell her to get on her knees and...

No! Don't go there. Not unless you want a semi while talking to her.

At the rate my body responds to her, an image like that would conjure up a full-on erection.

She's looking at me with such a sweet and innocent smile, even though I don't deserve it.

I can't help but let myself give in with my own smile. "You didn't seem like the type of person that likes to give up control. I figured I needed to be a bit more forceful than a simple offer."

She put her hand up in an attempt to stifle her laugh. I want to rip her hand down and tell her to never cover such a beautiful sound. "I've heard that before. I suppose you would've been standing there for a while if you didn't just come right out and say it like that. I need more of that in my life."

"More men telling you what to do?" I question, not sure where she's going with this or maybe my mind just can't get out of the gutter with this one.

"No! Geez. More people forcing help because they know I have trouble accepting it."

I rub the back of my neck. "Oh, that. Well, maybe you should work on just being more accepting of help."

She bites her lip and eyes me up and down. "Thanks, Mr. Obvious. Do you want me to suggest what you should work on?"

I throw my hands up in defeat. "I'll pass on that. Thanks."

I notice a nice farm-sized table set up in the kitchen.

"You got a new table?" I point out, noticing it wasn't there before.

"Yeah, I needed somewhere to work this summer."

She already has her laptop set up, and papers spread about.

"Well, I'll let you get back to work. Is it gonna be a problem that I'll be working around you today? Most of the work I have to do is in the kitchen."

She waves her hand in the air. "No problem at all. I'll just pop on my headphones. Let me know if you need anything."

"Good deal."

I start to move things around the kitchen as I bring in pipes and tools. It doesn't take me too long before I start to cut holes around the first floor, making a mess as I go.

I hope she doesn't kill me after all the scrubbing she did in the house. I try to sweep piles of drywall dust as I go so she doesn't have to see too much of a mess. Another thing I never do for others. Mess is part of the work, and I generally don't worry about it until the end of the day.

Luckily, even though I'm working near her, I get lost in the work for a bit.

After about an hour, I can feel the sweat start to run down my face. The sun is beating down through the windows. I'm in the foyer as I try to get the pipe that runs upstairs replaced. The patch I cut is a bit higher, making me have to get on my toes to get it secure.

I steal a glance out the window at the lake but notice her eyes on me from the kitchen table. Well, they are zeroed in on my stomach where I feel my shirt riding up.

She is lost in some thought right now. When she realizes I'm watching her, she sits up straight and quickly looks down at her computer.

I smile to myself, then get back to work.

Busted.

She was totally checking me out.

I like that she can't help but have her eyes on me. There's this lost part of me that I feel like her presence is awakening. It's been dead for years. I know it's dangerous for that part to come alive—I'm still a battered, bruised man.

On the other hand, it feels good.

After working to get this pipe in, the damn thing is struggling to go in. I realize I need a different tool that I think I left in the kitchen. I turn around to go grab it, but as I start to walk there, I stop in my tracks.

Charlotte has her headphones on and is mouthing the words to some song that must be playing. She has clearly gotten lost in the song and forgotten I'm here.

Her shoulders begin to move as she really gets into it. I creep over to the island and lean against it as I continue to watch the show.

The longer I watch, the more dramatic her dancing gets. It's frickin' adorable and sexy at the same time. I love getting a glimpse at her with her guard down. I hate that she has to forget I'm here for her guard to come down.

It takes about a full minute before her eyes meet mine. A look of horror flashes across her face.

She rips off her headphones, while I continue resting against the counter, arms crossed, and a huge grin on my face.

"How long have you been watching?" she demands in a piercing voice.

I shrug my shoulders. "Long enough to see a pretty good show that you just put on. That must be some song you've got on. What are you listening to?"

"None of your damn business. That's what," she fires back.

I laugh to myself. "Aww. Don't be embarrassed. It was a great performance."

She sighs. "And to think I was gonna be nice and ask if you wanted to have lunch if I ordered something."

That intrigues me. "That was thoughtful of you. Just so you know, if you asked, I would've said yes."

I don't give her the chance to reply. Instead, I push off the counter and grab my tool, then head back to the foyer.

The pipe is giving me hell, but I eventually get it in.

All I have left to do now is the second-floor bathroom.

I grab my tools and start bringing everything that I need up-stairs. Once I get set up in the bathroom, I hear footsteps approaching. I'm on my hands and knees under the sink but I turn my head to see Charlotte leaning against the doorframe.

She looks slightly amused.

"You know, I thought plumbers were supposed to be old, fat, and have their ass crack showing every time they were in that position."

I smile over my shoulder. "Can't do anything about the old and fat part."

Her eyebrows raise. "Oh, but the ass crack thing is still on the table?"

"It'll cost you extra," I say with a wink.

Her head falls back as she lets out a laugh. "Nah, I guess I can't afford the good stuff. I'm on a tight budget. Anyway," she takes a breath, then continues, "I think I'm over the embarrassment of being caught dancing and singing to myself. Still interested in that lunch?"

"I could go for some food," I tell her.

"Cool. It's on me. I'll go order us some sandwiches. Anything you don't like?"

"No, I'm not really that picky."

"I'll let you know when it's here."

"Thanks, Charlotte."

After she's gone, I take a deep breath that I must've been holding in.

Get a hold of yourself, man. She just asked you if you were hungry.

I know that's what it seems, but it feels like more than that. It feels like she is extending some kind of olive branch to me despite the way I've treated her since she's been back. There's an obvious attraction between the two of us, and part of me thinks it's dangerous to spend time in her presence. But the part of me that's drawn to her doesn't give a shit. Whatever it takes to keep feeling the way being around her makes me feel.

I work as fast as I can under the sink, wanting to get these pipes done before lunch. After that, all I will have to do is work on the shower, and I'll be done.

Just as I'm twisting the connector on tightly, I hear familiar footsteps coming up the stairs.

"Hey," she says as she appears in front of me. "Firstly, food is here."

"Alright," I put down my pliers and look up at her, "and secondly?"

"Secondly, can you please, please, please put the water back on? I have to pee so bad."

She begins bouncing from one foot to the other.

I chuckle to myself as I stand up.

"Yeah, I think I can manage that. I'll run downstairs to turn it on, then meet you in the kitchen."

I walk past her and start to walk down the hall.

"I thought you said you'd run downstairs?" she says, hot on my heel.

"It was a figure of speech. Do you really need me to run?"

"I have had to pee for hours, Asher. I *need* you to run," she says with urgency.

"Or I could just take my good old time and walk slower," I say as I take my step at a glacier pace.

"Asher! This is not funny. I'm gonna piss myself in front of you if you don't hurry."

A loud laugh that I barely recognize escapes me. "You do know that you can pee in the toilet without the water on, right? You just have to wait to flush."

With that, she shoves me into the banister and takes off downstairs toward the bathroom.

"I can't believe you didn't tell me that."

Her voice fades as she runs further from me. I walk the rest of the way to the kitchen with a huge grin on my face.

There are two boxes sitting on the counter from a great bakery down the street which also sells some amazing sandwiches.

My mouth waters just looking at the boxes as I wait for Charlotte to return.

When she walks back into the room, I can't help but take in the effortless way she carries herself. She isn't trying to impress anybody. You can tell she walks with her head held high but in such a down-to-earth way.

"You feel better?" I ask as she strides up to me.

She lifts an eyebrow at me. "Now you wanna play nice?"

"I'm nothing but nice."

Her heavy lashes that shadow her cheeks fly up. "Is that a joke?"

I look to the ceiling as if to ponder for a second. "Yes, I believe that was."

"Good. I was worried people in your life haven't been honest with you. You are definitely not nothing but nice."

"Oh, trust me. I've been told a time or two it wouldn't hurt to be nicer."

"I see you don't take people's advice very often."

I grab one of the bags of chips and open it up. "Hey, I've got your water running again. I'm helping you out on your deck. I think I'm plenty nice."

"Come on. Let's go eat this food outside. We can talk about your manners later."

We grab our boxes of food and our drinks and head outside. Tall trees around the backyard provide some much-needed shade from the hot summer sun and even offer an occasional light breeze.

"Thanks for getting the food. This place has great sandwiches," I tell her as we take a seat.

"No problem. It's the least I can do for getting this all done for me so quickly."

I unwrap my sandwich, take a bite, and lean back in my chair as I stare out at the water. I don't think I've ever been back here on this deck, aside from the other day with her. The view is something else. I could never afford a house like this on my own.

I'm shocked she wants to sell it. It's a complete gem.

I'm not sure how long we sit in silence eating, but when I look back in her direction, she's staring at me.

"What?" I ask.

She shrugs her shoulders. "I don't know. I guess I'm just wondering when you were going to acknowledge that we know each other or ask how I've been."

"Do you want me to ask you how you've been?"

"It's the polite thing to do."

"Okay," I put my sandwich down and look directly at her. "How have you been, Charlotte?"

She straightens herself with dignity. "Well, I don't want to answer now. It's not genuine. You're only asking because I said something."

I lean back, elbows on my armrests. "That's fine. You don't have to answer the question if you don't want to."

I pop a chip into my mouth and watch her as she eats her sandwich, trying to ignore my stare.

She doesn't last long.

"I've been fine. All in all, I can't complain too much. Life has had its ups and downs, but that's to be expected."

I bob my head, trying to act indifferent to her words even though I don't agree. I don't think we should have to expect life to have such low points. Life shouldn't crush you until you can barely breathe.

"What about you? How have you been the last decade?" she asks innocently.

I chuckle bitterly. "That's a loaded question."

Her head falls to the side as she watches me with interest. "You're different than I remember."

"That's a fair observation." I take another bite of sandwich as I let her probably compare me to the old version she remembers. No doubt she doesn't like the version she sees now.

Her eyes fill with curiosity. "Last time I was here, you were in a pretty serious relationship with that woman. I can't remember her name."

My body goes stiff and rigid. "Lauren."

"Lauren, that's right. I guess you two didn't work out?"

"We got married, actually." My stomach churns at the mention of her name.

"Oh, I see." She seems thrown off and nervous to push any further.

"She died two years ago from cancer."

Her entire body deflates. "Oh my god! Asher, I'm so sorry. That's awful."

I nod my head. "I stay busy with work and my daughter. Not much time to think about it."

"You have a daughter?"

I realize how little she does know about my life since she's been gone. I guess I figured my sister had already opened her big mouth and filled her in.

"Yes. Brielle. We call her Brie. She's three."

I take the final bite of my sandwich, desperate to get out of this conversation before it gets too uncomfortable and real.

"Well, I should get back to work. Thanks again for lunch."

Her eyes are sharp and assessing as she watches me collect my garbage. "Okay. It was nice to talk with you. Let me know if you need anything."

"Will do."

I walk away and take a deep breath as soon as I'm alone in the kitchen.

I hate when this topic comes up. It reminds me why I like my privacy. New relationships invite questions. Questions bring up scars that are better left hidden from the world.

Chapter Seven

Charlotte

"Wow. I haven't been in this place in so long," Layla says as she walks through my house.

She brought lunch from her restaurant, which I can smell from the bag in her hand. I'm excited to see what she has in there, but it's distracting me from what she's saying.

"I know. Doesn't it feel so weird to be back in here?" I respond.

"It looks exactly the same. Minus the huge holes in the walls and no furniture."

I laugh. "Yeah, your brother said he has two men coming out tomorrow to patch up the drywall."

I lead her outside to sit on the deck again for lunch. I'm slightly obsessed with the view from here. It's magical. I spent the entire evening sitting out here after Asher left, mostly reflecting on my conversation with him.

"How are things going? So far, it's just the water that's been repaired? What else is on the agenda?"

She starts to pull out some to-go boxes. When I see one of them is her calamari, I may slightly freak out.

"I'm sorry. I want to answer your questions, but my brain is short-circuiting with the knowledge that your calamari is sitting right in front of me."

She cracks up. "Dig in. Here," she hands me a plate, "I brought a couple of things so we could eat a little of each."

"I'm in on all of them." I scoop up some of each dish. "Anyway, your questions. Things are going better now. It was a little overwhelming when I first got here, with the water issues and all. Next on the list is the deck this weekend, then I think the floors. I'm gonna start painting the walls as soon as the drywall is fixed."

"Yeah, I'm sure it was a lot to walk into this with no real idea what you were in for. So, you're working on the deck this weekend?"

"Yep," I reply before I take a bite of calamari. "Sanding and then staining."

Layla halts. "Oh, you're going to sand this entire thing on your own?"

"That was the plan until Asher insisted on helping me. He seems to think I can't handle it on my own."

"Well, hiring him for the job is a good idea. That's a ton of work."

"Oh, I'm not hiring him. He offered to help free of charge."

"Really? He offered to help you all weekend?" she asks, seeming shocked.

"Yeah," I say with a shrug.

She leans back in her chair with a strange look on her face. It's making me feel uneasy.

"What?" I ask.

Her shoulders lift non-committedly. "Nothing. Just doesn't sound like him. That sounds more like the old Asher."

That piques my interest. I can't help but press her on the subject. "Yeah, I've noticed he is definitely not the man he was the last time I saw him."

She smiles. "You mean the man you had a massive crush on?"

"What? You knew?" I can't believe she never told me she knew. I feel slightly mortified.

Her head falls back with laughter. "Are you kidding me? I lost count of the times I would be talking to you while you were too busy drooling over him and had no idea I was even in the room."

I cringe a bit. For some reason, I thought I was stealthier than that.

"I was so shocked when I first saw him again, and he was just so...different. But now that I know what happened, it makes a lot more sense. I feel so bad for him."

"How do you know what happened?" she asks me.

"Oh, he told me while we were eating lunch the other day."

"You two were eating lunch together? What world are we in right now?"

I don't know what she's freaking out about.

"It was no big deal. He was working hard on the house. I offered to treat him to lunch."

Layla is looking at me with interest. "But he ate it with you? And was willing to talk about Lauren? That is not like Asher at all. He is a closed book when it comes to Lauren."

I don't know what to do with that information. It makes me feel oddly happy that he's willing to do these things with me that he normally wouldn't.

Okay, I can't let that go to my head. I'm already desperately trying to tell myself I don't still have a crush on him. "Anyway, the deck project will hopefully be done by the end of this weekend. I haven't talked to him about the timing of the rest of the projects."

"Well, I'm excited to see it all when it's finished. I forgot how much I loved the view from this place."

I look out at the water and instantly feel my body relax. "I know. Same. It's so peaceful."

We finish the rest of our meal, catching up on the past ten years. It's so nice being here with her, laughing and joking around like time never passed.

"You should come out with me and Avery this weekend. I'm sure you'll need a stiff drink after spending the entire day with my brother," she says as we walk our garbage into the kitchen.

She grabs her purse, and I follow her to the front door.

A night out with them sounds like fun. I could use that—I haven't had any fun since I found out about my father.

"That sounds perfect. Just let me know the time and place."

"You got it." She leans in and wraps her arms around me. "It was so nice to see you. I'm so glad you're back in town."

I sigh into her arms. "I'm actually kinda glad I'm in town, too."

We pull away from each other.

"I'll be in touch. Good luck with Asher this weekend," she says, then winks at me.

I'm not quite sure if it's a joke or am implication of something. Either way, I laugh it off and let her leave with her own ideas on the situation.

I walk back into the house and sit at my massive kitchen table.

When I touch my laptop mouse, the screen comes to life. Instead of getting straight to work, I start to think about Asher.

My mind has been spinning since we had lunch two days ago, and he told me about his wife.

I can't imagine what it must have been like to have a baby and lose the mother so soon after the birth. The thought alone makes my chest tighten.

I can see how that would rock your world and tear you apart. His anger and bitterness make complete sense now. That can make you question everything and leave you broken.

I feel a little guilty for the number of times I had watched him work when he didn't know I was looking. Minus the one time he caught me literally ogling his stomach when his shirt pulled up. It's his own damn fault. He shouldn't be that hot.

But here I am, objectifying him while he's just trying to do his job and support his family. Then again, I pulled a few smiles from him, and the winks he gave me felt like...something.

He laughed, too—a real laugh that made my heart flutter, knowing that I was the reason for it. Well, he may have been laughing at me having to pee so badly, but still.

But I can't let myself get all wrapped up in his charm. He's a single dad who has to prioritize his daughter. Dating him would mean being open to the possibility of becoming a mother to a little girl who deserves everything.

Why am I even thinking about this? It's like seventeen-year-old me interpreted a wink and a laugh as a marriage proposal.

I shake my head in an effort to erase these ridiculous thoughts.

What I need to do is focus on getting the house ready to sell by the end of the summer. That's what I came here for, and yet I feel myself falling right into the life I had before I left. From now on, I'm going to focus all my efforts on this house.

No distractions, especially not Asher Williams.

Chapter Eight

Asher

Who would've thought that having Charlotte Bates back in my life would cause such a tidal wave of changes in me?

She's made my hard armor crack one too many times in a matter of a week. Not only that, but I can't close my eyes without picturing her smile or her sexy-as-sin body.

Now I'm standing on her front porch with my equipment, and I actually feel something similar to excitement at the idea of seeing her again.

My hand lifts on its own accord to knock on her door before I'm mentally ready.

It swings open quickly. I swallow hard, lift my chin, and boldly look her directly in the eyes. The attraction is as powerful as the first day we met again a week ago, if not stronger.

"Hi." She smiles at me. "Come on in."

I follow her into the kitchen just like I did the other day.

"I see you brought your own stuff to work with?" she says as she points to the equipment in my hand.

"This is a slightly more powerful electric sander. Based on your little incident last weekend with yours, I think I should be the one who controls this one."

With both hands on her hips, she fails at her attempt to disguise her annoyance. It makes me smile.

"We'll see how you do with that one today," she cracks back.

It looks like she's conspiring something in her head, and I don't have a good feeling about it. She has no idea the power she has over me.

"What do you say we get to work?" I suggest before we get into it with each other.

It's like we're constantly trying to piss the other one off. Although, each time we try, there is a sexy undertone to the conversation that feels like foreplay.

If we ever had sex, I think it would be a cross between anger and passion. Damn, it would be something else to feel that tight body of hers all over my hands.

Luckily, she starts walking outside before my brain can settle too long on the image of what sex with her would be like. There's no doubt in my mind that I will be picturing it tonight when I'm lying alone in my bed. I've thought about it every night since the first day I showed up on her doorstep.

When we make it to the front porch, she turns to me.

"Alright, macho man. Tell me what to do."

I roll my eyes. I know there was no compliment in that comment. "I think I'm gonna send you to the back deck. You think you can work on sanding the banisters back there without getting into trouble? I can use my high-powered machine to cover the rest of the deck floor since it's a larger area."

"Yes, I can handle the railings, asshole."

She starts to walk off in the direction of the back deck.

"What's up your ass today?" I shout before she disappears around the house.

"You and your ego," her voice echoes before she's out of sight.

I chuckle to myself. I'm glad telling her about Lauren hasn't shied her away from treating me any differently. I feel like most people in town tiptoe around me, afraid I'm going to break any moment. Or maybe they're just afraid I'm going to snap at them. Either way, her attitude is refreshing to be around.

I scan the front portion of the deck that still needs to be sanded. It's really only about one-third of the deck floor. She did get pretty far up here, but the back deck is giant. I think about her losing her balance and falling on her stomach when she caught a glimpse of me without my shirt on. It makes me smile just thinking about it. If she only knew what the view of her body does to me.

Once I find the outside outlet and get the sander plugged in, I begin to plug away.

My sander has an attachment that I can place in the center of it to place a rod, so I don't have to be on my hands and knees. This allows me to move it around like a vacuum and save my back. But it does do a number on your arm muscles and abs. It takes a lot of muscle to keep the thing in place and direct it where you want it to go.

There are some two-by-fours that seem too far gone to salvage by sanding. They're split with large gouges, making them a safety hazard.

After I sand everything, which takes roughly an hour, I bring new two-by-fours up to the porch and begin to replace the damaged ones.

The morning flies by as I work on the front. I keep plugging away even though every five minutes, my brain tries to come up with an excuse to walk around to the back and see her. My body is so aware of her presence. I can't imagine how it would react if she ever touched me. Fuck, I want her to touch me.

Like it's perfect timing, I'm finally done sanding the front. I unplug my sander and walk around the house to the back, where I find Charlotte working hard on the railings. She's about halfway done with them.

She must spot me in the corner of her eye because she switches her sander off and turns around.

"Nice work," I tell her as I survey the section in front of me that is now free of any prior stain.

She winks at me. "Thanks. Who knew a woman could do this work without injuring herself?"

I smirk. "Well, when there's not an insanely attractive man with no shirt on distracting you."

She bites down hard on her lower lip as if to try and stop herself from saying something she may regret. Her eyebrows come together as I see her glare at me with such scrutiny.

I chuckle to myself as I set up the sander.

It's just so easy to mess with her. She doesn't disguise her emotions very well. A quality I find to be absolutely endearing, especially seeing her make the futile attempt to hide it.

I'm used to women who will say whatever they want, whenever they want, with little or no regard for how it may affect others.

They say it's in the name of being honest, but honesty can only take you so far. Eventually, you have to own up to the fact that you're just being cruel. One thing I've learned over the years—intention matters.

If the words you are saying are said with a negative intention, you *will* get a negative response.

I get lost in my thoughts as I begin to sand the back deck, starting in the far corner away from Charlotte so I don't interfere with her work.

When I finish the section in the corner, I maneuver the sander around to start in the other direction. I steal a glance in Charlotte's direction and see her slowly reach down and grab the bottom of her tank top with her hands, then she pulls it up and over her head.

She is just in her shorts and sports bra. This sports bra is smaller than her other one, too. Her breasts are popping out of the top so deliciously I can barely catch my breath.

I don't exactly know how it happens, but I'm so caught up in watching her like she's my own personal strip show that I think I loosen my grip on the sander. It takes off on its own clear across the deck.

"Watch out," I scream as it makes a beeline directly for Charlotte.

She lets out a high-pitched squeal as she scurries out of the way.

"Asher! What the hell?" she says as she hides behind me. Her hands reach for my biceps, fingernails digging in as we watch my machine banging into railings.

"Shit. I'll get it. Just stay back."

I follow the cord to the outlet and pull it out quickly. The machine slowly comes to a halt in front of us, landing with a thud on its side.

While I'm still trying to gather myself from the commotion, Charlotte's laugh ripples in the air.

I cock my head to the side, watching her erupt in this giant fit of laughter.

"I'm sorry. Did you get distracted when I took my shirt off? Did you lose control of your equipment? Maybe we should call in a professional to help us with this deck because clearly, you're in offer your head."

Her smile reaches across her face. Then it dawns on me—she did this on purpose, and she's thrilled that it worked.

I take several strides in her direction, anger emanating from me. I don't know if I'm angrier at her or myself for being so distracted that I could have possibly let this happen.

Next thing I know, I'm closing in on her with only the smallest fraction of air between our bodies. She cranes her head to look up and meet my eyes. Her smile fades as she takes in my disposition, my labored breathing.

I notice that her lips are full and the perfect shade of light pink. They are begging for me to taste them, to punish them for what she did.

The smile on her face fades. It's clear that the energy has shifted to something more dangerous. Her eyes fall to my lips, and her breathing matches mine. We are both caught up in this thing between us that seems to make us powerless to stop it.

My gaze slowly slides down to her breasts, sending shivers of excitement through me.

I suddenly can't remember why it would be a bad idea to kiss her. It's all I can think about, and she's making no attempt to step away from me.

My body leans in as my head moves closer to hers. She licks her lips in anticipation. My hand rests on her hip as I start to inch in closer and closer.

Her eyes begin to flutter. When my mouth is only a breath away from hers, a noise coming from the tree makes both of us jump.

"What was that?" she whispers with a hint of fear in her voice.

I step away from her, realizing I almost kissed her without considering the repercussions. She's my little sister's friend. I can't play with her heart, knowing that I'm not capable of keeping it safe. Safe from the anger and pain that I hold in my own heart.

"I think it was a squirrel," I say with a heavy voice as I take a step away from her.

"Oh." Her body seems to relax. "Okay."

Silence falls between us, neither of us knowing exactly what to do next. My hand grips the back of my neck and squeezes.

"I think we should get back to work if we want to get this finished this weekend," I tell her, not knowing what to say or do next.

She looks away from me quickly, then nods her head.

"Yeah. Good idea."

We both move toward our areas of the deck in silence and get back to work. My brain is still reeling from the fact that I almost kissed her.

My body feels wound up from the desire that was coursing through me. The adrenaline is making me want to turn around and finish what we almost started.

Dammit! I need a distraction.

I glance down at my watch. Thank God! It's lunchtime. A perfect excuse to take a break and reset.

"Hey," I say as I walk over to her. She powers down her sander and looks up at me. Shit, I still want those lips on mine. "I'm gonna go pick up some lunch for us. I'll be right back."

She gives me a hesitant smile. "Okay. Thanks."

I practically run to my truck and then slam the door shut as soon as I hop in. My head falls back against the seat as I try to calm down my erratic breathing.

"It's fine. You almost kissed her, but you didn't. Nothing to worry about," I whisper to myself.

When I return with the food, I'm feeling slightly better about what almost happened. So, we almost kissed. The important thing is that nothing happened. We just need to plow past this and forget about it. As long as I remember the reasons why it would be a terrible idea, I should be safe.

I walk around the house to the back deck to find her sitting down with a drink in her hand.

I hold the bags of food up as I approach. "Should we eat inside?"

We had to move the tables and chairs off the deck so there isn't anywhere to sit. Plus, it's a hot day. The air conditioning would feel good.

She nods her head and I follow her in. Once we take a seat at the table, I give her the sandwich and chips I got for us.

"Thanks," she says as she unwraps the foil.

"No problem. You treated the last time."

I'm glad I went to get some food. The tension feels like it's already cut in half. I think we can push passed this.

She takes a bite and stares at me. "Yeah, but that's because you're doing all this work for me. Not only are you working for free today, but you've paid for my lunch."

I smile. "Keep it in mind next time you call me an asshole."

She chuckles. "You're an anomaly. I can't quite figure you out."

"Well, ask me something then."

"What?" she asks with confusion.

"If you want to know something. Ask," I say before I pop a chip into my mouth.

She leans back in her chair. "Hmm," she says as she continues to think. Then she smiles. "What's your daughter like?"

I raise an eyebrow. "That's what you wanna know?"

She shrugs her shoulders, looking slightly embarrassed. "I've been curious. Does she look just like you? Walk around with a grumpy face to match her father's?"

I chuckle at the thought. "Not at all. Brielle is the epitome of joy. There's no room for anything but happiness when she's in the room."

She rests her chin on her hand, seeming oddly interested in hearing about my daughter.

"What else?" she asks. "Does she talk a lot?"

"She doesn't stop talking. She doesn't form long sentences, but they're long enough to understand. It's been so fun being able to finally talk to her and have her talk back."

She giggles. "You're gonna feel differently about that talking back when she's a teenager."

"Uh, I know. I'm gonna fail so miserably trying to parent a teenager."

"Somehow, I doubt that. But you have plenty of time before you need to worry about that."

We continue to talk about Brie, and she tells me more about her job working for the NFL. I'm a little bit, or majorly, jealous of the fact that she has been to a Super Bowl before and of the box seats she gets whenever she goes to a game.

After we are done, we decide to get back to work so we can be done by five. The rest of the day goes by without any incidents. We get the sanding done so that we can focus on staining tomorrow. I was also able to replace more two-by-fours on the back deck.

On the drive home, my brain takes me right back to when I almost kissed her. The way she looked in her sports bra and shorts. It was hard as hell to ignore how good she looked in them the rest of the afternoon, but I somehow managed. It was hot as hell, and I didn't want to ask her to cover herself up.

I did consider getting even and taking off my shirt again but I figured one of us could actually get hurt next time if the sanders kept getting away from us. We're clearly both in over our heads with this powerful attraction.

Chapter Nine

Charlotte

"So, where exactly are we going tonight?" I ask Layla while she lies on her bed, looking at the ceiling.

"It's a bar in the historic district of downtown."

"What's the vibe? I don't know what to wear," I say as I watch her lay like a starfish.

I look through my bag of packed clothes—skirts, dresses, shorts—a whole array of things to try on. I'm not exactly in the mood to get too dressed up. It was a long day of sanding, and my body is aching.

"Umm, it's a bit more on the nicer side, but not too nice."

I look over my shoulder. "That isn't helpful at all. What are you going to wear?"

"I don't know. Avery just texted and told me she invited the guys, so I'm still trying to get over my frustrations on that."

"What guys? Why are you mad about that?" I'm still trying to figure out the dynamic between everyone here.

She sighs. "Avery is dating Kyle. He's one of my brother's friends. You remember him? I'm not sure if you ever met any of my brother's friends."

I try to think back to his friends, but I don't know that I ever met any of them. Then what she says registers, and my stomach flutters. "You mean your brother is coming tonight?"

"I don't know if he's going, but I do know that means Josh will be there."

"What's up with you two? I haven't been around long, but enough to tell there's some animosity there."

She lets out a huff. "You could say that again. Josh is just a man whore. He has yet to grow up. It's annoying."

I look at her with curiosity. I don't know why him being a man whore would get her so worked up—unless there was something there between the two of them. "Has anything ever happened between you two?" I ask.

"Nothing of importance," she says vaguely, waving her hand.

Hmm. Interesting. She clearly has feelings for him, and she didn't say that nothing happened between them. But I can tell she is not going to admit it right now, so I let it go.

More importantly, there's a chance Asher might be there tonight. I'm not sure if I'm excited or not. If it weren't for that damn squirrel this afternoon, I think he may have kissed me.

I shouldn't want it to happen, but dammit, I do. The way he was able to make my body feel on fire from just his eyes on me was something I'd never experienced.

I can't even imagine what it would be like to have his mouth and hands on me.

Just the thought of it makes my body come to life.

Okay, that does it...I'm going for sexy tonight. I'm not even going to pretend it has nothing to do with Asher. It has everything to do with him.

I reach into my bag and pull out my white, shimmery crop top, pairing it with some jean shorts, and then I slip on black heels.

"Damn, girl. You look hot," Layla says as she gets off the bed. "You looking to get some ass tonight?"

I giggle. "Just want to feel good tonight. It's my first night on the town since I've been back."

"Well, mission accomplished. You look smokin'." She starts to look through her closet as I pull out some gold jewelry to go with my outfit.

"What are you going to wear?" I ask.

"Well. I think you set the tone for the night. I guess I'm going sexy."

She pulls out a nearly backless red top to go with a pair of sexy black shorts.

"Nice," I tell her as she steps into her shorts. "You look sexy as hell."

"Girl. It doesn't feel like a decade has passed since we've hung out. I feel seventeen again, and we're about to try and sneak into some bar together."

I laugh. "I know. Only this time, we won't be taking shots and puking all night."

"Speak for yourself," she says with a wink.

Oh, geez. Tonight may get crazy.

When we are done, we hop in the car that we scheduled to pick us up at eight. I start to wonder if Asher really might be there tonight. Then I think about the fact that he's a single dad and just spent the day with me.

There's no way he's gonna be there. I hate how disappointed I feel. This is a man who is struggling to raise his daughter, still dealing with the loss of his wife, and I'm not even staying here for good. He should not be occupying so much of my brain space.

It only takes fifteen minutes to get to the bar. We step out just when Avery is walking in.

"Oh my gosh!" she says enthusiastically as she walks up to me. "I can't believe you're back!"

I run into her arms. "It's so nice to see you again," I tell her as we squeeze each other.

"Tonight is gonna be so much fun. The three of us together again," Avery says. "Come on, let's go in."

I look around at the place and it's really cute. There is an outside patio that wraps around the entire building with string lights above.

I follow Avery through the building, past the main bar, and back outside, where she finds a section of outdoor furniture that is set in a circle.

"Here we go. This should fit everyone," she says as we all take a seat around the center table.

"So, I hear you're dating one of Asher's friends, Kyle. How long have you two been seeing each other?" I ask.

"It's only been a couple months. I know this one over here isn't a fan of seeing her favorite person more often." Avery gestures to Layla who sticks her tongue out at us.

I giggle at her immaturity, although I can tell she is joking.

"There's my girl," a deep voice bellows from behind us. I turn around and see Josh and the other familiar faces I met the other night at the café walking up to us.

My heart begins to quicken with excitement. As they get closer, I notice one face is missing from the group.

Asher.

My entire body deflates like I just found out my favorite candy was getting discontinued. Maybe I need to set my sights on a man tonight. Clearly, I have it bad for Asher, and that needs to change.

The guys begin to pile in the seats around us.

Kyle sits next to Avery and gives her a big, extended kiss that might be going a bit too far in public.

"Eww. Get a room," Layla says what, I'm sure, everybody is thinking.

Avery blushes while Kyle just winks at Layla, seemingly proud of his obvious affection for his girl.

"I'm surprised to see you're willing to brave being around this crowd again," Josh says to me from the couch adjacent to me.

I smile. "Aw, you guys weren't too bad. We'll see how tonight goes. I may just all of a sudden have a jam-packed schedule the rest of the summer," I joke.

Josh laughs easily, making me feel so comfortable in this group. I really need to talk to Layla about what happened between them. I just can't see anyone not liking this guy.

The waitress comes over and takes everyone's drink order. Since it's a warm night out, I decide to do a strawberry margarita.

"Oh, that sounds yummy!" Layla shouts from the other couch. "I'll change my order to that."

Josh rolls his eyes at her.

"Do you have a problem?" she glares at him.

"Must you always be so indecisive?" he remarks.

"I'm decisive when it counts," she replies.

I just sit back and watch them go back and forth, not sure if they realize there's anyone else around them. They seem lost in each other.

"Oh, yeah?" he says. "Like when?"

She crosses her arms over her chest. "When it comes to men."

His face turns cold as he glowers at her. "Whatever," he mumbles to himself.

As soon as my drink is brought out, I take a huge gulp to ease the tension in my body. The first sip feels so delicious going down. I really needed this night out.

I sit back with my drink and listen contently to the chit-chat back and forth between the group.

"So, you're saying that you don't think we needed to draft another offensive lineman to give our QB more time in the pocket?" Josh asks the group animatedly.

I assume he's talking about Atlanta. That's usually who people around here root for, and he's right.

"Nah, man. We needed another good receiver," David combats.

"You're insane!" Josh says with frustration.

"Actually," I step in. "He's right. Your O-line is terrible. You could have all the top receivers in the world, and it wouldn't matter unless you protect your quarterback and give him time to make a play."

The group falls silent. Josh looks at me and then back at the guys with confusion.

"She works for the NFL," Layla says proudly.

Somehow, when a girl knows sports, men look for a reason. Women can't just enjoy it without drawing attention, which pisses me off, but I'm used to it.

"Is this seat taken?" a familiar voice drifts through the air, causing my skin to break out in instant goosebumps.

When I look up, Asher is standing to my right, looking ridiculously good in his jeans and dark blue shirt. He raises an eyebrow in question when I look at the empty spot next to me and realize he's talking to me.

"Oh, yeah. Of course," I say quickly.

His smirk makes me wonder if he knows the effect that he has on me. There's not much space on the couch. When he takes his seat, our bodies touch from our shoulders all the way down to our legs.

My eyes close on their own accord as my body lets out a shiver.

"You cold?" he whispers in my ear. The heat of his breath is almost too much.

I don't know how much longer I can take these feelings that his presence evokes. This doesn't feel like the silly little crush I had on him a decade ago. This feels different.

I distract myself by downing the last of my margaritas and then ask the waitress for another one as soon as she appears.

"Charlotte, I can't believe you work for the NFL," Avery says. "That is so cool. How long have you worked there?"

"Three years. I work in the marketing department."

"Do you get to go to games?" Paul asks with a hint of jealousy.

I chuckle. "Yes, I get to go to games."

"You got any suite tickets for us this season?" Paul says with a wink.

Asher fidgets next to me, then puts his arm around the back of the couch, encasing me in. "Let's not try to use Charlotte for her connections the second time we've met her. Huh, Paul?"

Paul shrugs his shoulders as if it's not a big deal.

"How often does that happen to you?" Asher asks me while the others talk amongst themselves.

With his arm around me, our faces seem to be only inches apart. His body is leaning in toward me with no care for my personal space.

It's distracting.

He's distracting.

I have to remind myself he asked me a question.

"You mean, do grown-ass men beg me for football tickets regularly?" I say with a smile. "Yes, they do."

He matches my smile. "That must get annoying."

"Eh, I'm used to it."

His eyes study mine. I can't tell what he's thinking, but the longer he looks at me, the more I feel the need to fill the silence.

"I'm surprised you're here. Where's Brie?"

He looks a bit amused by my question. "Were you wondering if I was gonna be here?"

I roll my eyes. "Get over yourself."

When he smiles, I notice the creases around his eyes. They show the years that have gone by since we've last seen each other, but they are fitting on him. "I had dinner at my parents' house when I went to pick up Brie after I left your place. Since they are watching her again tomorrow, they suggested she just spend the night."

"Ah, I see. So, Daddy has the night off."

His eyes turn dark. I realize how that just came off. I've never found the whole 'daddy' kink particularly alluring, but it seems anything is where Asher is concerned.

"I do have the night off," his voice says gruffly. "Are you happy I'm here?"

Before I can answer, Layla interrupts. "Charlotte, what do you say we play a round of cornhole?"

She gestures to the area of grass that has the game boards set up.

I need to get ahold of myself. Getting away from Asher's close proximity is a must right now.

I stand up. "I'm down."

"Nice. Who wants to play us?" she offers to the crowd.

"You in?" Josh looks at Asher.

Asher smiles up at me.

Dammit! There's no getting away from him. "Yeah. I'm in."

Layla looks at me and rolls her eyes. On our way to the boards, she whispers in my ear.

"We need to beat these motherfuckers."

My eyes open wide in surprise. "Yikes. It's not just a friendly game of cornhole?"

She shoots daggers at Josh, who is holding the cornhole bags and beaming at Layla.

"No," she says harshly.

"You wanna stand next to me, Layla?" Josh asks, still sporting his wide grin.

"I say you mess with him," I whisper in her ear. "Just start saying sexy things and touching him. I promise you that man wants you. It'll totally throw him off his game."

She laughs out loud. "Girl, that's a fabulous idea. And I say you've got a man standing right beside him who totally wants you. Maybe we both can cause a little chaos tonight?"

She winks at me then stops the waitress and orders us both two shots.

"Liquid courage," she says to me. "Alright, Joshua. You ready to get on your knees and beg me to take it easy on you?"

"Sure, and while I'm down there, if you want me to do anything else," he says to her.

Asher finds me on our side of the boards.

"They think I'm an idiot," Asher whispers to me.

"What are you talking about?" I ask.

He looks over at Josh and Layla who are now fighting over what color bean bags they play with.

"Something must've happened between them. They clearly have history, and they think I don't know."

I smile up at him. "Asher, it's clear that they don't even know there's something between them."

"Charlotte, we're the lucky blue bags," Layla screams. "No thanks to this asshole who made me rock-paper-scissors over it."

Oh, geez. Between Asher's close proximity and these two, I'm thinking I'm gonna need more than a couple of shots.

Speaking of, just as we start the game, the waitress brings us our drinks. I order another strawberry margarita while Asher orders a beer.

I take the first shot right away, then place the other one on the high-top table next to me.

"I didn't realize it was going to be a shots kind of night," Asher says, then throws his bag.

I look at his biceps flex as he tosses another one, then grabs the other shot and shoots it back.

"It's been a long day," I tell him.

He throws his last bag. While Layla and Josh take their turns, he turns to me. It's so unnerving having all of this man's focus on me.

"Was it long because of who you spent it with or what you were doing?" he asks with interest.

The shots must be already going to my head because I feel myself stepping closer to him. I know I shouldn't, but my body seems to be in charge at the moment.

I lean into him, feeling the slightest touch of our bodies brushing together. I think I hear a sharp inhale coming from his mouth, but I'm too affected to be sure.

"Maybe a bit of both," I say seductively.

Or I think it comes out seductively. That could be the alcohol making me think there's something there that isn't.

"Your turn, guys!" Josh shouts from the other side. "Or do you two wanna keep giving googly eyes at each other?"

Asher steps away from me, and my body instantly misses his warmth.

I throw my bags. One slides into the hole while two of the other three land on the board. Layla shouts in excitement while Asher follows suit with his first bag in the hole. On his final throw, he needs to land it on the board, or we get a point.

I once again find my eyes focusing on his arms, the way his muscles flex while he holds and tosses the beanbags.

His bag lands on the board but slides off onto the grass. Layla is celebrating and getting in Josh's face.

My hands come up to his arm and wrap around his bicep.

Dammit, he's strong! My insides quiver, thinking about what he could do to me with his strength. I take one hand off his arm and rest it on his stomach.

"I believe I beat you on this round," I say, goading him.

I hear the beanbags slamming against the board a foot away from us, but I couldn't care less if we are winning.

Just when I think Asher is gonna pull away, he surprises me by leaning into my touch.

He looks down at my hand that is resting on his stomach then brings his eyes back to mine.

"You better be careful, Charlotte. I'm not a perfect gentleman, and you're poking the bear."

I should heed his warning—it's the smart thing to do...but I don't. Instead, I let my hand fall a couple of inches south.

I wish there was nobody else around us. His body tenses, and his face tells me he is close to snapping.

Instead, he steps away from me and grabs his bags off the board. I try to compose myself but end up downing the rest of my margarita while he takes his turn.

The rest of the evening starts to blur together. What I thought was going to be a relaxing evening with friends took a vastly different turn.

Chapter Ten

Asher

I knock on the door, waiting for her to answer. Last night was not what I expected. It went from innocent stares to Charlotte not being able to keep her hands off me.

At first, it was almost impossible to stop myself from letting my hands linger on her body. Then she got drunk, and the rest of the evening was me making sure my friends kept their distance from her, especially Paul.

I'm not an idiot. I see the interest in his eyes. Just thinking about it makes me want to punch his face all over again.

Luckily, the door opens, and her beauty distracts me from my anger.

She's in a baggy t-shirt and shorts. Her hair is on top of her head, and she still manages to take my breath away.

I smile. "Good morning, sunshine."

I walk in without her invitation and begin to whistle. She follows me into the house, groaning behind me.

"Why are you so chipper this morning?"

I turn around and can't help but grin at how adorable she looks.

"Are you not feeling well this morning? Could it be the shots? Maybe the margaritas?" I joke.

She looks like she wants to kill me. "Let's just get started."

I follow her through the sliding door to the back deck. She has the supplies waiting for us to begin staining. I'm somewhat impressed she was able to be up and ready for me this early. She wasn't completely hammered last night, but she was definitely a bit tipsy.

When she leans down to grab a brush and winces, a protective side of me surfaces.

I appear quickly by her side. "What's wrong?" I ask as I reach out for her and pull her back up.

"Nothing. Just thought I might get sick. I'm okay," she says, though her ghostly appearance suggests otherwise.

"That's it. You need to go inside and lie down." I start to take a step toward the door, but she stops me.

"No, you already came here. Your parents are watching, Brie. I can't cancel."

"Who said anything about canceling?" I reply. "You go lie down, and I'll get this done. It's just staining. This is the easy part. I'll have it done in a couple hours."

She looks like she wants to fight it, but I raise an eyebrow, daring her.

Her shoulders sink in defeat. "Okay. Thank you."

I nod my head. "My pleasure. I'll come check on you in a bit."

While she goes inside to relax, I pull out the stain and begin to mix it up. Visions of how she looked last night begin to creep into my mind. Her long, tan legs in those shorts, emphasized by her heels. Every time she tossed her bean bag, her shirt would move in a way that revealed her black lace bra.

I felt like such a creeper, but I couldn't look away.

Then when she couldn't stop touching me, I thought I might actually sport a stiffy in public like a damn teenager. Her hands were glued to my body every spare second during our cornhole game.

And fuck if mine weren't lingering on her as well.

This is such new territory for me. Not even when I met Lauren did I have such a powerful physical reaction. She was beautiful, stunning even, but I was so focused on impressing her and being the man I thought she wanted, that I don't think my body had time to be so responsive.

With Charlotte, it's like there's some connection between our bodies. It feels like they know each other, and when they touch, it's charged with something that cannot be tamed.

Eventually, I let my mind get caught up in the work. The smooth strokes I apply feel therapeutic as I focus on going with the grain of the wood. It's so satisfying to see the plain wood instantly pop with just the stroke of a brush. When I stand up to stretch my back, I realize I'm already halfway done with the staining.

I take a quick look at my watch. It's been two hours. I better go check on her to make sure that she is doing alright.

I throw down the brush and rag that I was holding and walk into the house through the back door.

The first thing I take notice of as I walk through the foyer and up the stairs is that the drywall is all patched up. I had the guys come immediately to make sure she could start to feel like there was progress being made. I didn't want her alone in a house with holes all around her.

This house is huge. I'm sure taking on this project on her own is daunting. I make a mental note of the things that I can do to ease the burden. I could easily change the light fixtures for her, which would instantly give the house a more modern feel.

I walk down the long hallway until I find her bedroom door at the end. I use the word bed loosely, as it's just a cheap metal frame with an air mattress on top.

She is sound asleep, her gray comforter pulled up to her chin. Just looking at her makes my heart skip a beat.

I sit on the bed, hoping I don't pop this damn mattress in the process.

She rolls onto her back, arms dropping above her head. I wait to see if she will open her eyes, but her breathing evens out, and she remains asleep.

"Charlotte," I whisper gently.

Her eyes flutter open. I watch her look around her room and then back to me.

"How long have I been sleeping?" she asks softly.

"A couple hours. I just wanted to see if you think you could keep down some lunch. I'm gonna go grab something. Maybe some soup or a small sandwich?"

She moans. "Ugh, I can't even think about food."

I notice her face is red, and she starts to shiver. When I lean in to put my hand on her forehead, she's burning up.

"I think this is more than just a hangover, Charlotte. You're burning up."

"I feel awful," she croaks.

"Okay. You stay in bed. I'm going to go to the pharmacy, see what I can grab. I'll pick up some soup on the way back."

I tuck her into the covers just like I do with Brie when she's sick.

"You don't have to do that," she mumbles under the covers.

"Of course, I do. You are in no condition to do it yourself. I'm already here and going out to get lunch. It's really no problem."

She sighs with her eyes closed. I wish I could do something more for her. I wish I could crawl under the covers with her and hold her.

"Thanks, Asher. Maybe you're not a huge asshole after all."

I smile. "I'll be back soon. Call me if you need anything."

Without even thinking, I lean forward and kiss her forehead.

What the hell was that? Why did I just do that?

Instead of sticking around for her reaction, I stand up and bolt out of the room.

I make my stops as quickly as possible. I don't like the idea of her lying alone, feeling miserable without anything to help ease the aches.

As soon as I get back to her place, I put the soup in the fridge and head up to her bedroom with the medicine.

She is still sleeping, so I put the medicine on the nightstand and feel her head again. She's still burning up. I don't want to wake her, but I would really prefer to give her something.

"Charlotte," I whisper.

When she opens her eyes, it seems to take her a second to orient herself as to where she is and why I'm there.

"I brought you some medicine," I tell her as I reach for the bottle on the nightstand. "I talked to the pharmacist. She said you should start with this and continue taking an anti-inflammatory for the fever."

"You talked to the pharmacist?" she asks softly.

"I didn't know exactly what to give you, and I wanted to make sure I gave you the best chance at getting some relief."

I realize how insane I sound. We don't know each other that well, and here I am, talking to a pharmacist for her and acting like a concerned partner.

I pour the medicine into the cap and hand it to her. She sits up onto her elbow and grabs the cap from me to take down the liquid, which, based on her reaction, must taste repulsive.

"Before you lie back down, take these two pills for the fever." I grab the medicine and open the bottle of water next to her.

She grabs them and takes a couple of swigs of the water.

"I'll keep the water and medicine right here for you. There's soup in the fridge that you can heat up at any time. I'm gonna go back outside to finish the deck. I'll check on you before I leave."

"Thank you, Asher. I don't know how I'm going to repay you for all of this."

"Just focus on getting better. No need to repay me."

I head back downstairs and get to work on the deck floors. I should be able to finish in an hour. It's a simple brush that looks like a mop and can coat it quickly.

I race through it as quickly as I can, then text my mom to let her know I'll be there to pick up Brie soon. When I go upstairs to say goodbye to Charlotte, I decide against waking her up this time.

She needs her rest. I'll just text her later to see how she is feeling. This time, I resist the urge to kiss her on the forehead.

"Is there a reason why you are hogging your own daughter from me?" Eric asks while our dinner is cooking in the oven.

I kiss the top of Brie's head while she scribbles her purple crayon all over her paper. She's making a castle, apparently. I've learned to just go with whatever she says she's coloring. One time, I looked too long, too hard to try and see it and she ended up in tears. It broke my heart. Now, everything is instantly beautiful.

"I haven't seen her much this weekend. I miss her, and she's mine, so I call dibs."

"What were you doing all weekend?" he asks.

"Oh," Layla raises her hand, "I know."

"Is there a reason you're raising your hand like the nerd in school who's excited to answer?" Liam asks Layla.

"Because I *am* excited. Asher here spent the entire weekend with my friend Charlotte."

I try to ignore her while I watch Brie switch to a pink crayon and continue her scribbles. I know Layla, and she's going to say something intrusive.

"You spent the entire weekend with a woman?" Eric asks curiously. "Just like... helping her?"

This time, I can't help but stare Layla down, but she smiles at me like she's proud of herself.

"I helped her sand and stain her deck. Layla is definitely acting like a child right now."

"Sure, you helped her with her deck. But you were also out with us at the bar last night, and the two of you couldn't stop touching each other."

"Damn. Asher getting back out there. Who would've thought we'd see the day? She must be special to get you to finally loosen up," Liam jokes.

"He's gonna have to go for it before someone else does, like Paul. I heard him saying he wanted to ask her out," Layla says.

I shudder inwardly at the thought. I try to suppress my anger in the guise of indifference, but it's too strong. I don't like the idea of anyone else with Charlotte, especially him.

I kiss Brie's head, lift her up, and place her down on the seat, then walk over to the oven. After I pull out the lasagna, I slam the door shut.

My siblings watch me begin to pace around the kitchen. I'm brought back to that night when I found out about my secret, and my life changed. I became this hard, cynical man that I am today. Instead of saying anything, my family knows to keep quiet and let me be. The anger settles after a while, and I'm able to make it through dinner without any more conversations about me and my personal life.

Once they are gone and Brie is asleep, I decide to text Charlotte to see how she's feeling.

Three hours later, I'm lying in bed, having a hard time falling asleep. She never texted me back, and my brain is producing all of these things that could be wrong.

What if she had a seizure from too high of a temperature? And I'm the asshole who left her alone in that condition. It would be my fault.

The rest of the night, I spend tossing and turning, hardly getting any sleep.

Chapter Eleven

Charlotte

I don't want to get up and go to the bathroom. I've been lying in bed for hours, trying to ignore it, desperately trying to fall back asleep. My body aches and I'm alternating between being extremely hot or miserably cold.

Finally, accepting defeat, I throw the comforter off myself and go to the bathroom.

I'm back in bed within minutes, bundled up in my blanket. I can't believe this is happening. I don't even know where I could've picked this up. I barely go anywhere.

Whatever, it doesn't matter. I just feel horrible that Asher came over yesterday and worked on the deck all by himself.

To top it off, he took care of me. I'm not sure if it was real or if I dreamt it, but I think he kissed my forehead. Maybe my temperature made me hallucinate.

A noise from downstairs grabs my attention. I grip my comforter that's bundled around me.

Was that the door opening? Is someone in my house?

There's no way. I'm definitely hallucinating from this damn fever. Then, the distinct sound of the front door shutting echoes from downstairs.

Okay, that was definitely the door.

In a panic, I try to decide what to do. I desperately search for my phone when I hear the footsteps coming up the stairs.

Holy shit. I'm about to die! I can't believe this is how I go out. In bed with a fever, never married, never able to become a mother. All the things I've never done in my life begin to flash before my eyes.

I never got to have my favorite hazelnut ice cream again since I've been back in Isle of Hope.

What a stupid thing to think when I'm about to die!

The footsteps are loud and quick, like whoever this is knows exactly where I am. This is a planned attack! Who do I know that wants me dead that bad?

I'm about to beg for mercy when Asher appears in the door-frame.

He looks angry and appears to be out of breath.

"Asher?" I ask in confusion.

He strides into my room. "You didn't answer my texts."

I push off my hands to lift myself up slightly higher.

"You texted me?"

He takes a seat on my bed like he's done it a million times, like his presence in my house, walking in without knocking, is completely normal.

"Like fifteen times. It's been twelve hours. I thought you were dead," he says while he reaches for my forehead. "You're still burning up."

I find myself leaning into his touch. His hand feels so good against my skin. It feels comforting.

"Have you taken any more medicine since I left?"

All I've done was sleep. I'm afraid to answer him, but judging by the look on his face, he knows my answer.

He huffs out a breath of frustration. I think I hear him mumble that he shouldn't have left me alone last night, but that can't be right. My health isn't his responsibility.

He reaches for the medicine on the nightstand and pours me another dose.

"I'm guessing you also didn't eat the soup that I put in the fridge."

"Asher, all I did was sleep and avoid getting up to even pee. No, I didn't eat the soup. Plus, it's boring in here. There's no T.V. or anything for me to do. Sleeping was my only option."

He looks around the room and then back at me.

"You stay here. I'm gonna run to the store. I'll be right back."

I don't get a chance to ask him where he's going before he is out of my room and running down the stairs.

This man is seriously infuriating. He is making my brain spin in circles trying to figure out what he's thinking. And who storms into someone's house, shoves medicine in their mouth angrily, then turns around and leaves just as quickly?

My body begins to shiver again. I hate having a fever; it's such a contradicting concept to have my body sweat and yet feel so cold.

Since I must've slept twenty hours straight, there's no going back to sleep. I lie here with my eyes closed, thinking about this mysterious man who is taking care of me.

It's been a rollercoaster ride since we've been back in each other's lives.

When I hear the door open downstairs, I at least know now that no one is here to murder me.

It takes him longer than expected to get up the stairs, but when he walks into my room, he's holding a large box and grunting. I don't even know what to think.

"What is that?" I ask hoarsely.

"Just a small dresser. I figured I could set it up in here. You could put some clothes in the drawers and a T.V. on the top."

"Oh my gosh. Asher, when I said that, I didn't intend for you to go out and buy me a dresser. I don't even have a T.V. here."

He grunts again as he opens the box. I'm shocked to see it's a really nice dresser. It only needs the hardware put on and the legs twisted at the bottom; everything else is in one piece. Nothing cheap comes already put together.

"I happened to have a spare at my house. Still in the box and everything. I stopped at home to get it."

Before he moves to get it out of the box, he turns to me. "I can tell you want to say something, but it's not worth it. This was an easy fix. Not only are you sick, but you're also going to be here all summer. You need something to keep you entertained."

With that, he goes back to work, leaving me with nothing to say. I guess if I can't argue with how over the top this is, I might as well enjoy the view.

Watching him lift it out of the box, his arms flexed to the max, makes me forget about the aches and pains all over my body. At one point, he lifts his shirt to wipe off a drip of sweat from his forehead. A glimpse of his abs makes my panties get the slightest bit of moisture in them. Even when I'm sick and in pain, this man can produce a reaction like this from my body.

After the dresser is ready and the hardware installed, he runs downstairs to get the T.V.

"I just realized I don't have cable turned on here," I begin as he plugs it in.

He chuckles, then looks at me over his arm. "You think I did all this and didn't think about that? I have a box right here where you can connect to the internet and access all of your apps."

Once it's all hooked up and ready to go, Asher shocks me by lying next to me on the bed with the remote. He opens up an app for me and then asks for my username and password.

He signs into my account and then starts to go through my recently watched shows and movies.

"What are you doing?" I ask while I lie next to him.

It feels so strange to be lying in bed with Asher, my teenage crush, like it's no big deal. I always pictured it going differently if we were ever in bed together.

I wasn't sick with a fever, and he wasn't lying there with a remote in his hand focusing on a T.V. instead of me.

Maybe I needed to be more specific with the universe when I asked to be in bed with this man.

"I'm curious what entertains you, Charlotte." He cracks a smile as he continues looking through my history. "You seem to enjoy light stuff with humor."

"Nice observation," I say sarcastically.

"Seriously, do you not like to mix it up with any drama or anything?" he asks as he continues to click through the app. He looks over at me.

I shrug my shoulders. "I like to be happy when I'm watching something. Plus, I really only watch something before bed. If I stir up too many emotions, I can't sleep."

He clicks play on the first season of one of my favorite shows.

"I've never seen this," he admits.

I'm super confused as to what's going on. Is he going to watch this with me in bed? He's acting like this is no big deal.

When he doesn't say anything or look like he's planning on getting up, I follow his lead and begin to watch the show with him. I guess this is happening.

Every time he chuckles at something, I feel my heart flutter in my chest. This man does something to me; he always has. I wonder if he always will.

That's a scary thought. Will I always react to him this way, even if I'm married and happy? Get out of your head, Charlotte. When you're married, you won't be living here and likely will never see him again. The thought alone of never seeing him again brings a pang to my chest.

I notice his breathing has gotten a bit heavier, so I steal a glance at him, hoping he doesn't catch me looking. His eyes are closed while one arm rests on his stomach and the other above his head.

He's sleeping. Asher is sleeping in my bed. I take the chance to look at him uninterrupted. My hand itches to run across his strong chest, which looks well-defined even through his shirt. His lips look so soft and full.

Well, I'm not going to wake him up. He is a single dad, after all; he's probably exhausted.

Instead, I watch the show and try to let my body rest. I still feel awful. The body aches are the worst, and I feel like I just ran a marathon. But after the first episode, I begin to shiver again.

My fever is back, and no matter how bundled up I am, I can't seem to get warm.

I look at Asher, feeling his warmth next to me, and move closer. The closer I get, the more the chill in my body begins to fade. I keep inching closer until my entire body is pushed up against his. Then I close my eyes and rest in the warmth of our body heat.

The next thing I know, I'm waking up wrapped in his arms. His scent surrounds me, a masculine scent. It's subtle but smells like a woodsy, smoky aroma.

I wiggle around to try and get comfortable, but his arms close around me tightly. I look up, and his eyes meet mine.

"You fell asleep," I say to him.

"I did," he replies. "You feeling any better?"

"Actually, I am." I notice my aches and pains are gone now.

"I think you sweat out your fever."

I have to think about it for a second, and then I notice that my shirt is drenched in sweat. I move my hand from resting on his chest.

I think I might die right here, right now.

"Oh my god! I sweat all over you."

I push myself off the bed and sit up. This is mortifying. Why did I have to sweat out my fever during the one hour when we were cuddling? Does the universe hate me? What did I do to piss it off?

Asher doesn't look phased at all. He sits up. "Yeah," he says slowly. "That's a good thing."

"But I sweat all over *you*," I say with emphasis. "That's gross."

He tries to hide his smile when he realizes what I'm saying. "Are you embarrassed?"

"Yes! That's it, you cannot stay in those clothes. What if I get you sick? You have a daughter you need to be healthy for. Get up," I say to him as I jump out of bed.

He follows me as I walk into the bathroom and grab a towel. Shoving the towel in his chest, I push him toward the shower.

"Here. Take off your clothes. Take a shower and let me wash your clothes."

He looks surprised. "You want me to shower here?"

"Yes! I sweat all over you. You need to get it off."

I'm honestly not sure why I'm freaking out so badly about this. It's just not how I pictured being in bed with him, and I'm desperate to rectify getting him all gross with my germs.

Instead of following my demands, he looks at me, slightly amused.

"I've gotten a woman's sweat all over me plenty of times."

"Well, this isn't because of sweaty, hot sex."

I lose my train of thought as I think of the two of us fucking so hard that we are sweating all over each other. My brain can't stop picturing it.

"Charlotte," his raspy voice pulls me away from my thoughts. His eyes are dark and serious. I feel like he can see through me; like he knows exactly what I am thinking about. "If it makes you feel better, I'll take a shower. Just stand on the other side of the door. I'll hand you my clothes."

He starts to walk me backward out of the door, then closes it, but winks before his face disappears.

Why do I always seem to make a fool of myself in front of him? He must think I'm crazy. Not only did I just sweat all over him like he was my own personal sweat towel, but I just demanded he strip naked in my bathroom and shower while I did his laundry. Then he makes me lose my train of thought with images of us naked together.

Although, he's the one who brought up sweaty sex.

When he opens the door to hand me his clothes, he has the towel wrapped low around his waist. I have never in my life felt every nerve in my body so active and alive.

Every inch of Asher is perfect. His tan from the summer just adds an element that makes him look like he should be on a magazine cover. Since I can't move, let alone breathe, he steps closer and places the clothes directly into my hands. Before he closes the door, he winks at me again.

I clutch his clothes in my hands and stare at the door for what feels like a creepy amount of time.

When I finally gather enough wits about me to move, I run down the stairs and throw his clothes in the washer on the speed cycle.

I'm disgusting. I can't believe I let him see me like this. Luckily, I have spare bathroom products in my travel bag. I grab it and run to the spare bathroom with a towel. I know I don't have long, so I take the world's fastest five-minute shower.

When I'm done, I switch his clothes over to the dryer. I walk into my bedroom in my towel to find something to wear, but before I can make it to my closet, the bathroom door opens.

There he is again in that towel. Only now, his hair is slicked back and wet. It brings a whole new level of sex appeal that has me losing all ability to speak.

"You showered," he says as he leans against the doorframe.

His presence feels like it takes up the entire room.

"I did."

I walk toward him.

Why am I walking toward him? What are you doing, Charlotte?

I'm standing right in front of him, taking in the muscles in front of me. Particularly stuck on the ones that extend from his hands to his elbows. They are flexed as his arms are crossed across his chest.

My heart starts hammering in my ears. When I look up at him, he is peering at me intently. He seems curious, amused by my obvious appreciation for him.

I start to think about all the times I pictured having him like this in this particular house. Now, here he is, standing right before me, giving me a challenging look like I don't have enough courage to do what I really want.

"I'm sick," I blurt out.

"Yes, you are," he replies with a cool, easy tone.

"I don't want to..." I begin but can't get the words out. "If I...my mouth has germs. They would get you sick."

Oh, shit. I'm totally screwing this up.

His eyebrows raise. "Your mouth could get me sick."

"But like...only if it was on your mouth."

His head tilts to the side as he watches me with interest. "Yes, your mouth on mine could get me sick."

Just do it. Say it! Take this opportunity—your dream man standing in front of you half-naked.

I take a deep breath.

"But my mouth on other parts of you would be fine," I say as I try to stand tall with confidence.

It's his turn to be speechless. I watch his throat bob.

"What are you saying, Charlotte?" he says with a raspy voice.

"I'm saying that I want to do something for you, something I've wanted to do since I was seventeen."

I'm tired of talking about it, and he's clearly not saying no. I move my hand and run it over the towel, feeling his hard length underneath.

His sharp intake of breath gives me the courage to continue. I walk into the bathroom and push him until his ass hits the counter.

"You've wanted to do what since you were seventeen? Wait, you wanted me at seventeen?" he asks.

I slide my fingers under the top of his towel, where it's holding it together, and tug until it falls to the ground.

It's my turn to lose my breath. His long, thick cock is huge as it bobs right in front of me. It's already hard and ready to be played with.

"Of course, I wanted you," I say, though I'm slightly distracted by how perfect every part of Asher is.

He seems a bit nervous as he fumbles over his words. "I had no idea," he begins as I fall to my knees. "I mean, I think I noticed you looking at me sometimes, but I never really thought it meant anything."

I wrap my hand around his dick and give it a good tug.

"Oh, fuck!" His head falls back in pleasure, and yet he continues to talk. "You were so young."

I watch him curiously as I circle my tongue around his tip. He starts to talk faster, more franticly.

"I couldn't let myself see you that way. It's not because you weren't beautiful."

He's still going when I wrap my lips around him and slide all the way down his shaft. He bites out a guttural moan.

"Because you were beautiful. So damn beautiful. But I was twenty-two at the time. Plus, I was seeing someone."

I pop off him. "Do you always talk this much when a girl is going down on you?"

He huffs out a laugh. "I don't." He runs his hands through my hair in the most delicious way, then grabs my hair and holds on tight. It's hot as hell. "You're just driving me out of my damn mind."

I smile. "Good. That's the plan."

Instead of wasting any more time talking, I slide my mouth back down his shaft, moaning as I go down. He tastes delicious.

He growls as he watches me. I begin to move up and down him in a slow, steady rhythm making sure I suck hard while gliding my tongue around him.

"Fuuuuck," he draws out. "You look so damn sexy taking me in like that, like you enjoy having my dick in your mouth."

I'm slightly confused by his words. I pop off him and talk in between licks around his tip. "Of course, I want to do this. I'm gonna be touching myself tonight thinking about this."

"What the fuck?" he replies as I take him back into my mouth until he hits the back of my throat. "Who the hell are you?"

Instead of answering with words, I show him. I show him what I've wanted to do for an entire decade.

He grips my hair so tight, my eyes begin to water, but the pain just makes the moment so much more intense...so much hotter.

"You keep taking my dick like a good girl. I'm gonna have to repay you," he breathes as he starts to thrust forward, making me take him deeper and deeper.

I knew it. I knew he would be exactly what I craved. No man has ever talked to me like this, but it's always been how my fantasies go.

I moan in appreciation as I look up at him. When our eyes connect, something powerful sits in the room with us—some kind of connection and understanding that what is happening is significant.

The thought of him returning the favor, of his mouth on my pussy has me frantically sucking with excitement. I add my hand at the base of his shaft, working it while I suck harder. I pull back to show some attention to his tip again. Sucking on it like a lollypop as I alternate between licking and sucking.

I bit of precum starts to drip out. I can't resist.

With the tip of my tongue, I ever so gently let the tip of my tongue glide along his cum, then begin to pull away, creating a trail of cum from his dick to my tongue.

His eyes grow darker as he watches. "You are fucking filthy."

I smile softly up at him, then lick his tip clean and swallow. I love seeing how affected he is by me. It's thrilling as it creates more enthusiasm as I continue to work him with my mouth. His groans become more desperate as I feel his dick tighten, letting me know he is about to come.

When he makes a move to pull back, I place my hands on his ass and shake my head back and forth.

He bites his lip as he watches me take down his release while he curses through his grunts.

I pop off him and gulp down the load of semen in my mouth.

"Charlotte," he whispers as I stand up. His hands cup my cheeks and start to trail a feather-like touch down my neck onto my shoulders.

As amazing as it feels, my body is also extremely weak. I haven't eaten in over a day and haven't stayed hydrated enough. Things start to look a bit fuzzy for a second.

"Are you okay, Charlotte?" he asks as he bends at the knees slightly to be eye level with me.

I nod my head. "Yeah, sorry. Just feel a little faint."

"When was the last time you ate?" he asks.

I shrug my shoulders. "Not since yesterday morning."

He takes my hand and leads me out of the bathroom, into the bedroom then pulls the covers of my bed back.

"Get in. I'm going to go warm up that soup for you."

I look down at him and smile. "You're naked."

He smirks. "I realize that. The most beautiful woman in the world got greedy with me."

"She's one lucky woman," I say as I lie down, closing my eyes.

He pulls the covers up to my chin and then looks at me gently. "I'm the lucky one, Charlotte."

With that, he walks out of my bedroom, leaving me wondering what exactly he means by that.

What just happened? Did I just initiate my teenage fantasy for a one-time thing? Is it going to happen again?

I want it to happen again. I want more. I want to feel his lips on mine. I want to feel his cock stretching me until I'm full.

I need to focus on getting better first. I can't believe my body gave out on me. I wish I could've seen what he would've done next.

Chapter Twelve

Asher

I'm not here for her. I'm here to hang out with my friends.

That's what I keep telling myself as I drive to the bar. It's complete bullshit, and I know it. All I've been able to do this week is think about the other day in her bathroom when she turned me into a rambling idiot.

It's been driving me crazy that I didn't get a turn to touch her, to taste her. I can't stop thinking about what she could possibly taste like or how she might look when she comes.

Is she as enthusiastic when she comes as she is when making me come? Because the way she eagerly sucked me off was unlike anything I've ever experienced.

My dick twitches at the thought.

But I know nothing can happen again between the two of us. That was a one-time thing. It's too dangerous to dip my toe in the pool of Charlotte. I'll want to submerge my entire body and never come out, and she's leaving soon to go back home to Cincinnati. I should be playing it safe with a woman who doesn't make my heart skip a beat. Someone I know I won't risk getting my heart stomped on all over again.

I park in the large field outside the bar. This place was formerly a large barn that was turned into a line-dancing bar.

The place is packed tonight. People are out on the large dance floor with their partners as country music fills the air. There are picnic tables along the perimeter of the dance floor and twinkling lights hanging above the entire barn.

The large barn doors are opened on all sides so you can walk out to the patios, which are also lit up with twinkling lights hanging from the large southern trees.

I scan the room, trying to find my group. I first spot Josh sitting on top of one of the large picnic tables. He's laughing at something David says while the rest of the group is scattered around them. When he leans back, I notice Charlotte talking with Layla.

Her bright smile makes my chest feel like it has a ton of bricks on it. It's hard to take a breath.

Her eyes meet mine from across the room like our bodies knew the other's presence.

I take long strides toward her, no longer concerned with telling myself I'm here for any other reason but her.

"Look who made it," Josh smiles up at me. "I'm not used to seeing you out so often." He looks over at Charlotte and then back at me with a knowing look. "I wonder why you're so social these days."

I shrug my shoulders. "Must be the good weather."

He smirks at me. "Must be. Well, if you'll excuse me, I need another beer. Want one, bro?"

I nod even though I want to slap him in the back of the head.

When he's gone, Charlotte looks over at me with a smile.

"You wanna sit down?" she looks down at the spot next to her.

I opt to sit on the top of the table where Josh was while Charlotte sits on the seat below me, slightly to the right. With my elbows on my knees, I lean down so we're closer.

"You look beautiful," I tell her.

Her cheeks turn a darker shade of pink. "Thank you."

"You seem to be feeling better."

"Much better. Thanks to you."

Taking care of her wasn't even a second thought in my mind. I'm just happy that she's doing better.

"Not a big deal. I hated to see you like that."

She casts her eyes downward before meeting mine again. My gaze drops from her eyes to her shoulders, then to her breasts. I can't help but take in all of her beauty, and her breasts look fantastic in her tight red tank top. A tiny glow crosses her face. She must know that her body makes me hot.

"Hey, big brother," Layla appears in front of me. "I thought you hated this place."

What is with everyone calling me out tonight?

"I never said that." I glare at her.

"Yes, you did. You said you hate dancing, and that's all everybody does here."

"You hate dancing?" Charlotte asks.

"I don't hate it. I just don't... like it," I say, loathing myself for sounding so insecure all of a sudden.

"He didn't always hate dancing. He used to be fun, but now he hates everything," Layla says to Charlotte.

I roll my eyes, officially annoyed with her presence. "Why are you still here?"

She winks at me. "Because you love me."

Josh returns with our beers. I take mine and we all sit around the table talking for a while. Paul and David, who were in the corner with some girls, have joined us and are seated on the other side of the table.

Avery and Kyle are chatting with Charlotte when a familiar song begins to play. The group starts to cheer with excitement. Avery and Kyle disappear on the dance floor, Layla grabs David, and Josh finds some random girl, like usual, leaving Charlotte, Paul, and myself.

Just as I'm about to say something to Charlotte about her renovations, Paul cuts in.

"You wanna dance, beautiful?" he says to Charlotte.

She smiles innocently at him. "Sure. I love this song."

I watch them walk away together, his hand resting on her lower back as he leads her to the floor. He whispers something in her ear that makes her head fall back with laughter. My hands ball up in fists as I watch him wrap his arm around my girl's waist.

It's just a dance. Calm down.

I take a swig of my beer, which now tastes stale and bitter in my mouth. My eyes never leave the dance floor, never leave Charlotte.

They begin to move together, smiling and laughing as the music plays around them. His hand, which was on her hip, has now taken up residence on her lower back.

Then I notice him pull her body toward him, molding themselves together.

He smiles seductively at her.

That. Mother. Fucker.

I can't take it. I can't watch him do this. He has some nerve after everything I've been through. Clearly, everybody else around us can see that I feel something for Charlotte. How can he be so blind to what's around him?

Maybe he isn't blind. Maybe he just doesn't care.

When I see his hand slide down further, practically groping her ass, I jump out of my seat.

I need to get out of here before I do something stupid. What Charlotte does is none of my business. I don't own her.

As soon as I'm outside on one of the patios, I lean against the barn. My head falls back as I close my eyes and try to take deep breaths.

It all feels like it's happening again, right in front of my eyes this time. The pain from Lauren's mistakes feels like I'm finding out for the first time.

My fingernails almost pierce my skin my from clenched hands—my attempt at deep breaths does nothing to calm down the fire inside of me.

"Asher," I hear a familiar voice.

I open my eyes to find Charlotte standing in front of me.

"Is everything alright?" she asks.

The song she was dancing to is still blaring through the speakers inside.

"What are you doing out here?" I ask, avoiding her question because, fuck no, I'm not alright.

"You looked upset then you just stormed off. I thought you might be angry," she says sounding concerned. "Are you okay?"

Her hand reaches out and grabs mine. I can feel the warmth of her skin on mine. Her touch sets my body on fire.

A simple touch of a hand has never made me burst into flames before, but I've never met anybody like Charlotte before.

What kind of person notices someone that's upset from across the room and leaves in the middle of a dance to go check on that person?

Someone like Charlotte, that's who.

An image of Paul with his hands all over her flashes in my head.

"I am angry," I admit. "I'm furious."

"Why?"

"He thinks he can touch you," I say as I point inside the barn.

"Who thinks they can touch me?" she asks with confusion.

"Paul!" I shout. "He thinks he can touch what's *mine*."

"Yours? You're saying I'm yours? You haven't even kissed me yet," she points out. "You haven't done anything to show me you want me to be yours."

That's easy. I can solve that in an instant. If that's all that's holding her back from letting me claim her as mine, challenge accepted,

I wrap an arm around her waist and pull her flush against me. Her sharp intake of breath mixes with mine. Our mouths are a fraction of an inch away from each other while my eyes settle in on her lips.

"If you're telling me all I need to do is kiss you to make you mine, then you have three seconds to stop me before I do," I say with conviction.

I hold my breath and wait for her to deny me, but it never comes.

Then she surprises me. "Kiss me," she whispers. "Make me yours."

That's all it takes. My mouth is on hers. I squeeze my arm tighter around her waist to push her against me and grab her cheek with my other hand. I tilt her head to the side so I can take further control of the kiss.

There's no slow build to the kiss; my tongue is mixing with hers, stoking the raging inferno building between us.

I feel her get on her tiptoes then feel her lips press harder against mine, a needy moan escaping from her mouth. Her hands fist my shirt, pulling me toward her even though we can't get any closer.

The groan I release in her mouth gets swallowed by her greedy mouth.

She kisses like she sucks my dick, with passion. My hands grab her ass and lift her up, then I turn us around and slam her back against the barn.

She screams into my mouth but doesn't falter. I'm not sure how long we ravage each other against the barn, but eventually, I slow it down.

When I pull away, our chests are heaving together in heavy unison.

"Wow," she whispers.

I smile down at her and then kiss her nose. "Let's get inside before everyone comes looking for us."

I don't want to stop, but I also don't want people out here making a spectacle of this when I'm not sure what it all means.

As we walk back inside, me following close behind her, my brain starts to mess with me.

Dammit! I let my anger and jealousy, my history, take over without thinking about the repercussions.

Of course, I want her to be mine. I'm clearly being ruled by my body whenever she is around. But I also don't know if I'm cut out for anything more than just a casual fling.

And I really don't want to hurt her. Nor do I want to find myself hurt at the end of the summer.

We get to the table where everyone has gathered again, only instead of letting Charlotte take a seat, I take her hand.

"What are you doing?" she asks as I lead her to the dance floor.

"I wanna dance with you."

I spin her around and then pull her body against mine.

"Is this just some alpha male thing where you just want Paul to see, or do you really want to dance with me?"

I look at her as I consider her words. "Can it be both?"

It's true, I want Paul to know who gets to dance with her, but I also want to dance with her.

I start moving our bodies to the music, and she seems to forget about her reservations. The strange thing is, I do, too.

I haven't enjoyed dancing in years. I haven't enjoyed much of anything in years except my time with Brie.

Charlotte is like the breath of fresh air that I haven't had, nor did I think I'd ever get again.

We laugh as we dance, following the crowd's two-step. I feel my-self smiling the entire time as we stumble over the dance, trying our best to keep up with the people who obviously frequent here regularly.

When the song ends, I grab her hand and walk us back to the table where everyone is busy chatting.

Layla winks at me, and I just smile. Normally, that would piss me off, her trying to imply that she knows something is going on, but I'm too happy to care.

I look down at my watch, realizing I need to get out of here. Ma is at my house while Brie sleeps, and I need to make sure she can get home before it's too late.

"I have to get going," I whisper into Charlotte's ear, who is standing at the end of the table drinking her beer.

"Already?" she asks with a sad look on her face.

I nod. "I have to relieve my mother from babysitting duty at my house. I wasn't exactly planning to come out tonight."

"What changed your mind?" she asks.

I smile. "I may have heard this pretty lady that I can't stop thinking about was gonna be here, and I wanted to see her. Even if only for an hour."

Her lips curve up. "I think you made her night."

"I'll call you, Charlotte," I say as I squeeze her waist and whisper in her ear, "Thanks for the dance."

I wave goodbye to the group and walk outside to the parking lot. I'm not sure what tomorrow will bring, but right now there are no shadows across my heart.

Chapter Thirteen

Charlotte

"I know, Mom. I'm not going to get carried away. I promise," I tell her over the phone as I hit send on my last work email for the day.

I want to start painting the walls on the first floor today, so I'm clocking out early. I just had to let my boss know. But I have an amazing boss who has been very understanding of my situation since my father passed away.

"I just don't want you to put too much time and energy into that house. I hate that you got left with the workload in the first place. If you need any money," she begins, but I stop her.

"No, absolutely not. This isn't your problem anymore. Plus, I haven't even spent that much. Layla's brother has his own contracting company. He's been a huge help."

Mom brightens up at the mention of Layla. "Oh, I'm so glad you are back in contact with Layla. You two were so close. Which brother?"

"The oldest, Asher." Even saying his name has my body getting tingles all over.

I walk over to my paint cans and tools, deciding where I want to start.

"Oh, Asher was always so kind. How is he doing?"

I smile to myself, thinking about all the rude shit he's said to me since I've been back.

"He's still as kind as ever, Mom. I'm gonna get started painting now. I'll call you soon. Love you," I tell her.

Once I'm off the phone, I put it in my pocket. I'm wearing black cotton overalls with a white bralette underneath. I wore them once to paint my place in Cincinnati and ended up getting paint on the legs, making them my official painting overalls.

I pour the cream-colored paint into the tray and grab the stick and roller from the bag. Once the roller is coated in paint, I begin rolling along the walls of the foyer. Knowing I have to paint this entire house from top to bottom makes the task feel a bit daunting.

My arms ache after rolling for thirty minutes from extending so high. But as I cover more surface and see how nice and clean it's starting to look, I get a bit more motivation. I know the end result will look amazing.

My thoughts continually drift back to Asher. I don't know what is going on between us. He kissed me on Saturday night, an earth-shattering, life-altering kiss, but I haven't heard from him since.

He said he'd call me.

I know it's only Monday, and he has a daughter to take care of. I can't blame the guy for being busy, but I also can't help my brain from coming up with all these reasons why he hasn't called. Maybe he realized he doesn't like me all that much or doesn't think I'm worth the effort.

What if he met someone else?

Before I can go down that rabbit hole in my head for the hundredth time, there's a knock on my front door.

I place the roller in the tray, careful not to splash the paint over the sides, then open the door.

My heart skips a beat. He's standing there leaning against the frame with one hand, looking like my fantasy come true.

Why does he look so damn good in his work boots, jeans, and white shirt?

A shy smile forms on his face. "Hi."

"Hi," I respond, still surprised he's here. "What are you doing here?"

He pulls at the back of his neck and then looks at the ground.

"I was just finishing up at a house nearby. I thought maybe I'd stop by and talk about what project you wanted to start next." He looks me up and down, then peeks behind me. "I see you decided to start painting."

I don't think he needed to stop by to ask what project is next. A phone call or text could've solved that. But I love that he's here, for whatever reason.

"Do you always make home visits to ask a client what project is next?" I ask.

I think his shy smile is my new favorite thing. "Some-times...maybe."

I giggle as I open the door. "Come on in."

He starts to look over my work, scanning the walls right here in the foyer, which makes me slightly nervous.

"I like the color," he says. "It'll look good against the floor stain you said you wanted."

"Thanks. I'm excited to see it all come together. Although painting this high is a workout. I didn't anticipate it to be this hard."

"Yeah, it can take a lot of muscle to get it done." He looks up at the high foyer walls and the long pole my roller is on. "I can knock the high parts of this foyer out really quickly for you."

"You don't have to do that. Don't you have to get back to Brie?"

He stares down at his watch. "It's only three. I have some time before I need to pick her up."

Then he grabs the roller and begins to roll with ease up to the ceiling where I could barely reach. Alright, so it seems like we're just gonna ignore the real reason he's here. He clearly can't bring himself to admit he came here to see me.

I'll go with it.

I smile to myself, secretly filled with pleasure that he wanted to see me as badly as I wanted to see him. A surprise visit is so much better than a text or phone call.

While he works on the top, I grab a small brush and start painting along the bottom of the wall where it meets the trim. There's no point in me not getting work done as much as I would like to just stare and ogle him.

At one point I have to crawl around him to get to the trim below him, but we seem to work well together. Every time I steal a glance in his direction, he's looking my way. Instead of owning it, he turns his head quickly and begins painting again.

Asher

Stop behaving like a middle school boy who's afraid to get caught staring at his crush.

I'm trying like hell to focus on the task at hand, but it's impossible when she's looking sexy as hell in her overalls with whatever lacy bra thing she has on underneath.

I can see her tiny waist, showing off her irresistible figure.

I watch her wipe her forehead with the back of her hand as she stands to stretch out her back, exposing the tops of her breasts even more, and something inside of me snaps.

I drop the roller in the tray, paint splattering everywhere, but I don't give a shit. I'm redoing these damn floors anyway.

Her eyes widen when she sees me take two long strides toward her. I grab her brush and throw it on the ground.

"What are you doing?" she gasps.

"I didn't come here to work. Okay? I came here to see you."

She smiles. "I know."

"I know something that you don't know, though," I say to her as I step closer.

She takes a step back, her breathing accelerating. "What's that?" she exhales.

"That I'm going to fuck you. Right here. Against this wall."

I don't let her get out another breath before I claim her mouth. I lift her in the air and press her body up against the wall. Her legs wrap around my waist as our tongues come together, proving how starved we both are for each other.

"We're gonna get paint all over us," she says as she notices her body slammed against a freshly painted wall.

I kiss down her neck. "Fuck the paint. I need to taste you."

"Oh gosh," she breathes as I kiss further down to her chest.

I stop and look down at her overalls. Our eyes lock as I slowly grab one of the straps and pull it down her shoulder, and the top left of her overalls falls, revealing her breasts encased in her white bra. It's see-through, giving me a peek of her pink nipple that's budding perfectly for me.

I momentarily forget about the other shoulder. I lean down and wrap my lips around her nipple through her bra. My tongue rubs against the bud. I groan into her breast, not able to hold back what she's doing to me. I feel all the pent-up energy slowly begin to release.

Her hand reaches behind my head and grips my hair, holding me in place as I suck on her through the fabric.

Feeling greedy, I tug her bra down and wrap my lips against her flesh. First, I give her light circles around her nipple then I bite down with my teeth, causing her to cry out.

While I continue my pattern of licking, sucking, and biting on one nipple, I yank down the other strap of her overalls and free her other breast.

I roll her nipple between my fingers until she is writhing in pleasure. Then I let her overalls fall to the ground. Her white lace panties make my dick even harder.

I look her up and down, baffled at how someone so perfect could want a damaged man like me.

Falling to my knees, I grab a leg and lift it up onto my shoulder. Her hips are raised, making her pussy eye level with me. Just where I want it.

Then I slide her lace panties to the side, revealing her glistening, pink pussy.

I'm so screwed. I'll never stop wanting this woman.

I look up at her as I take the first slow taste. My tongue starts at her entrance and ever so gently, moves up to her clit.

Her head falls back against the wall as her eyes flutter closed. A loud moan breaks free from her lips.

"Look down at me, Charlotte. Watch me taste you for the first time," I demand. "I want you to watch my tongue all over your pussy."

I grab her waist, one hand on each side, and pull her onto my mouth. This time I go straight for her clit, burying my face between her lips like a starved man. That's what this feels like. Like I haven't eaten a thing in years, and her pussy is my first taste of food.

Each lick and suck bring her closer to her release, but I never let her get there. It's far too sexy to watch her get all sweaty and needy with frustration.

I moan into her pussy, not able to hold back my own arousal.

She keeps rubbing herself all over my face, desperately trying to chase her orgasm.

"Fuck, please," she begs.

I stop and pull back. "Turn around. Put your hands on the wall."

"What?" she asks, sounding confused.

My eyes turn in at her questioning me. "I said. turn. around. Don't make me ask again, Charlotte."

She obeys my command this time without question, placing her hands on the walls while looking back at me.

Her ass is absolutely delectable. This is quite possibly the best view of my life. I grab her cheeks and spread her ass so I can see everything.

"Fuck, you are perfect, Charlotte."

When I look up at her, her eyes are on me as a faint blush forms on her face.

I lower my face and wrap my lips around her clit again, and I begin to suck her clit the way she seemed to enjoy so much.

Her moans are instantly back, her head falling forward against the wall.

I raise a hand and let it fall against one of her round cheeks, and a loud slap echoes in the hall.

"Shit!" she screams. I continue my assault against her pussy with my tongue, pulling back to spread her lips and push my tongue inside of her. She turns her head. "Do it again. Spank me."

I stop what I'm doing and look up at her. So, she likes to be punished.

Interesting.

With my eyes still locked on hers, I raise my hand and slap her again, this time harder. Her mouth falls open, but her eyes never leave mine.

My dick is uncomfortably hard at this point, but I'm only focused on her pleasure.

I smack her ass again, loving the red mark that is already evident.

I grab her cheeks and spread her again; this time, I lick her back entrance.

Her eyes go wide, but I can tell she likes it by the way she licks her lips as she watches.

"Has anyone ever tasted you here?" I ask as I pull back just an inch.

She shakes her head, and I go for honesty as well. "I've never done this before either. Does it feel good?"

She shakes her head up and down quickly.

"Good," I moan and lick her there again. "Cuz I don't want to stop."

Feeling like I can't get enough, I move my hands to her hips and push her ass into my face.

"Fuck, baby. It's so hot having your eyes on me while I fuck your ass with my tongue."

Her moans tell me she is really enjoying it. When she shimmies her ass in my face, it's my turn to moan.

I rub a thumb against her clit, and she starts to lose it. With my tongue in her ass and my thumb on her clit, she comes on a scream.

I pull back, still on my knees, and look up at her as she pants heavily.

I'm ruined. I haven't even sunk my dick inside of her yet, and I know it.

She turns around and leans against the wall, her chest heaving. I stand up and slam my lips down on hers.

"You've really never done that before?" she asks in between kisses.

"Never," I tell her.

She smiles as we kiss. I pull away from her. "What are you smiling about?"

She shrugs. "I like that you've only ever done that with me."

I smile back. "I'm open to trying more things that I've never done with you. Especially if it makes you happy." I kiss her lightly. "But right now, I need to fuck you."

She wraps her arms around my neck, pulling me in for another smoldering kiss. When her hand rubs against my length through my jeans, I groan into her mouth.

She unbuttons my pants, then slowly pulls down my zipper before she pushes my pants and boxers down to the floor. I kick off my shoes and free myself of my pants then pull my shirt off.

She shimmies out of her underwear so we are both standing naked.

I lift her up into my arms. "Wrap your legs around me, baby."

As soon as she does, I have her up against the wall again, kissing her with everything that I have.

"Shit," I say as I pull away. "I don't have protection."

"I'm on the pill, and I'm clean. It's been a while for me."

"I'm clean, and it's probably been longer for me."

"I trust you if you trust me."

I lean in and kiss her nose. "I trust you."

I line myself up at her entrance and push in only slightly. I have to take a second, as her pussy is already tightly gripping me. I push in another inch, continuing slowly until I bottom out.

Our breaths mix with each other as we adjust to the feeling of my dick stretching her. I pull out slowly, then push back in faster and harder.

My forehead falls to her shoulder.

"Baby, I'm not gonna last long."

"I'm right there with you," she whispers. "I promise."

Thank God. I grab her ass and hold on tight as I pull out and start to savagely fuck her. I'm lost in the sensations, the feeling of how tight she is, how wet she is, and how incredible this feels. I fuck her with everything that I have. We come apart together, sweating and breathless.

When I pull out, she unwraps her legs and stands on her own.

"I think we need a shower," she says as she surveys our sweaty bodies. "Do I have paint on me?"

She turns around, and I burst out in laughter.

"What?" she asks. "It's everywhere, isn't it?" She glances back at the wall. "Oh my gosh. That's my ass print on the wall."

I lose it even more, laughing harder than I have in forever as I see her perfect ass print on the wall. I reach for my phone in my jeans on the floor.

"What are you doing?" she gasps.

I open the camera and take a photo. "I need a picture of this. Come on, it's hilarious."

She folds her arms across her chest, then ends up smirking. "Send me the photo."

"You got it, baby." I throw my phone back down on my jeans. "Come on, let's go get cleaned up. I think you might need a little help."

I follow her up the stairs, trying to contain myself as I watch her painted backside sway.

When we get into the shower, she stands under the water and lets it wet her hair. I stand behind her in awe of how beautiful she looks under the spray of the water.

She takes a loofa and pours a healthy amount of soap on it then lathers it. She tries her hardest to try and scrub her back but it's just not enough to get the paint off.

I step under the water with her. "Let me help you."

I position her so the water is running down her back and start to scrub. It takes several minutes to get most of it off. I have to use my fingers to rub off the remaining paint. I then kneel down to try and get it off her ass.

Every time I try to scrub it with any force, she steps forward. "Hands on the wall," I tell her.

"That's what got us into this mess."

I chuckle. "No, I just need you to stop falling forward so I can get this shit off you."

She bends over and puts her hands on the wall. It's the most ridiculous thing I've ever done. Watching her in this position as I take a loofa to her ass cheeks that I can't help but start to laugh my ass off again.

"What?" she asks nervously over her shoulder.

"I'm sorry," I try to control myself and get back to work but can't. "I just don't think this is how I envisioned my first time with you."

She watches me over her shoulder as I try my best to scrub this damn paint off her ass without losing it.

Her laughter starts to fill the shower. "You're right. This looks fucking insane."

We both laugh hysterically for so long that I think I might stop breathing. It dawns on me that since Charlotte has been here, my life has been filled with smiles and laughs.

The thought is scary, but I also know there's no way in hell I can stop the train I'm on. It's going full steam ahead, whether the tracks are there to keep me safe or not.

Chapter Fourteen

Charlotte

"I'm so excited we get to do this," Layla says as we walk down the streets of Savannah.

"I know. You definitely need the night off. You work your ass off at the café. When's the last time you even took a vacation?" I ask her.

I see the guilty look on her face. "I haven't taken one since I bought the café."

"Girl, you need a trip."

She sighs. "I know. It's just so hard to walk away from the café and trust someone else with it. It's my life, Charlotte."

I nod, understanding her concern. Although, I can't quite think of anything in my life that I feel that strongly about.

What would it be like to be so passionate about something? I have my job, and I *love* it. But it's not like that for me. It's not my life, my entire source of happiness.

The scary thing is, right now, I can't remember the last time I've ever felt this happy. There's something about this place that makes my heart feel at home, but it's more than that. It's the man who owns my thoughts that is making the difference.

"Alright. This is the place my friend recommended." Layla opens the door to a fancy little Italian restaurant.

We are seated by the window overlooking River Street. The street is filled with people walking along the cobblestone, while the lantern lights set the mood.

"You up for sharing a bottle of red?" Layla asks.

"Sure. You can choose. I'm not picky."

While she scans the wine list, I look out the window again at the view. This place holds so many memories, so many incredible memories. I hate that I've tucked those memories away just so I didn't have to face the reality of what my father did.

Why was it so easy for him to leave me?

I shake my head. Don't go there tonight, Charlotte.

Layla orders the bottle and an appetizer for us, then folds her arms on the table in front of her.

"Okay, so...how has your time back in Isle of Hope been?" she asks with a smile.

"It's been good. I've actually been thinking about how happy I am that I was forced back here. It was just what I needed. I was in a bit of a rut back home."

She turns her head to the side. "Why?"

"Oh, just stupid boyfriend stuff," I say as I wave my hand in the air.

"Well," she says as the waiter pours our glasses of wine. "Seeing as that we have the entire night, and now some alcohol to ease the pain, I'd say you should catch me up."

I smile and lift my glass of wine. "To drinking while talking shit about exes."

"I'll cheers to that. I've got some shit I could air out, girl. You go first."

I take a large sip of my wine. "So, my most recent failed relationship lasted a year. It was such a cliche ending. Dated for a while, then when I wanted to know if we were headed somewhere serious, he freaked out and ended things abruptly. I felt completely taken aback. I thought, after being together for a year, it was a completely reasonable question to ask, especially given our age."

Layla leans back in her chair and gasps. "The nerve of the asshole."

I shake my head in agreement. "Yeah. It was a couple of rough months for me after that. That was about a year ago. I've kind of been on a bit of a break from men ever since."

"Interesting," Layla says thoughtfully. "And this thing between you and my brother?"

My body freezes. "What about me and your brother?"

She rolls her eyes but smiles. "Let's not pretend like there isn't something going on between the two of you. You guys disappeared at the bar the other night, then came back, and Asher all of a sudden wanted to dance for the first time in years. And let me tell you, the smiles on your faces while you two danced, I haven't seen him like that in a long time. Have you guys acted on this chemistry?"

My body shivers at the thought of me being the reason he wanted to dance again. After what he's been through, I love the thought that I could be the reason he is happy again.

I also don't feel like lying to Layla. It was never something we did before, and just because I'm with her brother, I'm not about to start now.

"Yes, we've acted on it."

She claps her hands together in excitement. "I knew it!"

I smile, excitement building that I finally get to talk about this with someone. It's been lonely trying to keep it inside when all I want to do is gossip like a teenager to my friends.

"Don't get too excited. I don't really know what's going on between us. It's only been a couple of times, and we haven't really discussed anything. I mean, he's a single dad and I'm leaving at the end of the summer. How could we make that work?"

Her face falls. "But he's been so much happier ever since you've come around."

"I know. Honestly, I've been happier since I've been here too."

"Then maybe you two can figure something out. What if you didn't leave?" she says hopefully.

"You mean, stay here in Isle of Hope?"

"Why not? You love it here, don't you?"

I exhale sharply. "I do love it here. But my mom is in Cincinnati. I can't imagine her ever wanting to come visit if I stayed in this house that must hold so much pain for her."

It's the first time the idea has come up, but the thought of decorating the place as my own, spending my mornings outside on the deck watching the boats go by with a fresh cup of coffee…it makes me kind of want that life.

"I imagine that would be tough for her, but you can't decide your happiness based on others. I'm sure she would be able to come around to the idea, if it really was what you wanted."

"Maybe. I don't know. I can't really think about that right now. I have to focus on getting the place done. Plus, Asher and I are nowhere near ready to talk about something like that."

Layla looks at me like she's contemplating her words. "There is something I wanted to talk to you about regarding Asher."

My stomach falls. "Umm...okay."

"It's nothing horrible. It's just..." she pauses, "he's been through a lot. The sudden death of Lauren, something none of us could have ever expected."

"I know, it's horrible. Losing your wife so young, and with a baby."

She sighs. "I don't know. I feel like there's more to the story, but he hasn't been willing to open up to any of us about it. He's different now, even from the way he was while she was sick and after she passed. It was months after she was gone that like...a switch flipped, and he became this bitter, angry man."

"Maybe it just took some time for reality to settle in before he became angry at the world for what happened. He could've been in a state of shock."

She seems to ponder my words. "Could be. I just get this feeling that there's something I'm missing. Either way, I just want you to be careful. I don't want to warn you away from him, just make you aware that he's been through a lot, and I'm just worried he hasn't resolved his feelings toward everything surrounding her death."

An ache forms in the pit of my stomach.

Is he still grieving her loss? Am I just a distraction?

It's only been a few short weeks, but knowing he used me to distract himself from the pain of his loss would ruin me.

But, if I'm being honest with myself, I don't get the sense that that is what is happening between us. It feels much bigger than that.

"I appreciate you telling me. I do. I don't think I'm at a point where I'm going to push him on his darkest feelings yet, but I know if things continue between the two of us, it's a discussion that will need to be had."

I do my best to move the conversation back to more optimistic subjects. Tonight is not about worrying about all the what-ifs in my life. Though I can't deny that her words play on repeat in my head throughout the rest of our evening.

Chapter Fifteen

Asher

"How's everything going?" I ask my flooring guy, Bret, who is currently sanding everything down at Charlotte's house.

"Not bad, man. This house is big with a lot of hardwood, but I'm making progress."

"Need a hand with anything?" I ask.

There's a stretch of silence. "Uh, no boss. I'm good."

I stumble over my words. Of course, he's good. He knows what he's doing, and I've never needed to offer him a hand with his work before. I'm just itching to see Charlotte and want to find any excuse I can.

I cough. "Okay. Umm...just let me know if there's anything I can do. I'll talk to you later."

I click off the phone and kick the gravel beneath my feet.

Idiot.

Ever since my night with Charlotte, it's all I can think about. She's all I can think about. I open my pictures on my phone and pull up the paint-smeared wall I took after we had sex.

I smile at it for what feels like the hundredth time.

"Fuck it," I say to myself, then open the door to my truck and hop in.

As I drive to Charlotte's place, I try to think of a good excuse to give Bret other than I'm falling hard for the owner of this place and need an excuse to see her.

Before I can think of anything, I'm pulling into her driveway. This is not like me. I am not the type to be clingy or desperate to see someone—I never was. And yet, here I am, walking up the stairs of the freshly stained porch, which looks out of place against the peeling paint on the house's exterior walls.

One thing at a time.

Before I can knock on the door, it flies open, and Bret is standing there with a stunned look on his face.

"Boss," he says with a questioning tone. "Everything alright?"

"Uhhh, yeah. I...uhhh...just wanted to see if I should maybe put another guy on the job with you and Harry so you can get it knocked out faster. You said it was a lot of flooring on the phone."

He scratches the back of his head as I walk past him into the foyer.

"Umm...no, I think I'm okay. We should be done with the sanding by Monday next week. Then I can move to the staining, which doesn't take nearly as long. Between me and Lance, we will have it done in a day."

I nod my head as I walk along. Of course, he already has Lance on the project with him. I knew that.

"Sounds good. You can get back to work. I have some other projects around here that I need to plan out with the owner."

"No problem. Catch you later."

He puts his headphones back on and walks out the door. Probably needs more sanding paper or something or maybe some privacy to bust a gut over my obviously desperate acts as a lovesick man.

I walk into the kitchen, but Charlotte's usual work setup is not at the table. Instead, she is sitting on a nice-looking outdoor couch with cushions. Her laptop is on her lap, and she is working with headphones on.

When I open the door and am greeted with a huge smile on her face, it feels like my heart skips a beat.

She pulls off her headphones. "Hey, you. What're you doing here?"

I shrug my shoulders, slightly embarrassed. "Just needed to make my rounds and check on the guys to make sure everything was going smoothly," I lie. "Thought I'd stop in and say hi."

"I'm glad you did." She stands up and walks over to me. "Did you already check on the guys? I think everything is going fine in there. It's a bit loud with the sander, so I figured I'd work outside for the day."

"Umm, yeah, I already talked to Bret. They should be done on Tuesday. I could make them work the weekend if you want it done sooner."

"What? No, they don't need to work the weekend. There's no rush."

We stand in silence for a moment. I watch her lick her bottom lip as her eyes land on my biceps.

Fuck this.

I reach for her hand and pull her body into mine, then kiss her pouty lips. My hands glide along her jaw as I take my time slowly working our lips together in unison. It's not rushed like our other kisses have been.

I know this can't lead to more right now since the guys are just inside. So, I just take the time to memorize the softness of her lips, the way they feel against mine, and the feeling of her body pressed against mine.

"I have a confession," I say in between gentle kisses.

"Yes?"

"I didn't actually need to come here today," I admit.

She pulls back and looks up at me. "What do you mean?"

I realize I don't want to dance around this with her. I'm sick of finding excuses to come over here.

"I just wanted to see you, but I didn't know how to say it," I admit, feeling slightly embarrassed.

She smiles coyly. "Really?"

"Yes, but I'm done pretending like I should be holding back. Clearly, I suck at it anyway and will eventually find a reason to see you."

"You don't need a reason." She wraps her arms around my waist. "You could just *want* to see me."

I rub my hands up and down her arms, loving the feeling of her smooth, silky skin.

"I want to see you, and this doesn't count. I have to head out and stop by another work site. One that I actually should be at right now if I wasn't so desperate to see you."

"When are you free next?" she asks.

I scratch the back of my head. "I've utilized my parents a lot lately for watching Brie. I don't know." Then I just blurt it out. "What if you come over tonight after she's in bed?"

It feels like a huge step. I've never had a woman over at my place before. That's my happy place, where I'm focused on being the best father that I can be. It's mine and Brie's sanctuary.

"I can come over tonight. Just text me the address and when I should head over."

I lean down for another kiss, drawing it out as long as possible. "Good. I look forward to seeing you."

I begin to walk backward to go around the deck back to my truck.

She smiles. "That wasn't so hard now, was it?"

"It's not so bad being honest." I wink at her. "See you tonight."

Chapter Sixteen

Charlotte

I reach for my perfume and squirt it on my neck. If there's one thing I make sure I carry with me everywhere, it's my perfume. The fastest way to kill the mood, in my opinion, is giving off an unfavorable scent.

I open my car door and make sure to close it slowly. I don't know how light of a sleeper Brie is, but the last thing I want to do is wake her up.

His house is smaller than I expected, but it's cute. As soon as I get to the door, it opens quietly.

Asher is standing there in gray sweatpants and a black shirt, barefoot and looking too sexy than any man has the right to.

I walk in past him into his private little world. He closes the door behind me while I look around. It suddenly dawns on me that this was probably a big step for him to invite me to his home.

There are toys in random places, scattered in corners, sitting on the coffee table. Pictures of his daughter are framed on the walls.

His hand reaches for mine, and he leads me through the kitchen to a door at the far end of the house, closing it behind us.

"Sorry," he says as he leads me into what appears to be the master bedroom. "Brie's room is on the other end of the house, so we should be good in here. I don't want to risk waking her."

"I get it."

He leads me to his bed and then falls onto it with little grace; it makes me smile.

He pats the spot next to him. "I know this isn't very romantic," he says as he realizes we just snuck into his room like we're teenagers.

I don't want him to feel bad. I love that he's letting me into his world. I kick off my shoes and fall in next to him, matching his clumsiness. "I think it's very romantic. We can pretend like we're sixteen and sneaking around."

His arm wraps around my waist and pulls me in. "We have to be quiet. My parents are in the other room," he whispers in my ear.

I let out a soft giggle. "I've never done this before. Will you go easy on me?" I say, feigning innocence.

He lifts his head, eyes dark with lust. "I can't make any promises."

Then his lips are on mine, hard and demanding. His lips sear a path from my neck down to my stomach as he slowly strips away my clothes until I'm down to just my underwear.

Lying between my legs, he takes one of them and pushes it up with his strong hand so I'm spread open for him.

He hooks his finger in my underwear and pulls it to the side, revealing myself to him.

"I've been dreaming about tasting this pussy again."

I squirm as I watch him take me in, my heart pounding erratically. When his thumb grazes my entrance and then rubs up along my clit with the moisture that he gathered, a moan falls from my lips.

"You're so wet for me already. Does it turn you on to know my parents are in the other room?"

Shit, he's good at this roleplay thing. I honestly had already forgotten about it.

I smile at him, a devilish grin. "I've always had this fantasy," I start. "Getting caught...being watched."

"Fuck," he whispers, then descends on me.

His lips and tongue know exactly what to do. The way he starts slow, tasting me, letting my need for more build until I'm squirming for more.

When he slides in a finger, I lift my hips off the bed because he hits the perfect spot instantly. His lips wrap around my clit, and he sucks—*hard*. Then he takes another finger and lets it run against my back entrance. When he finds my hole, he lets his pinky enter me slowly while his pointer and middle finger go in my pussy. Then he pumps his fingers in and out while continuing to give my clit all the attention it needs.

It makes me go off like a rocket.

I try to stifle my moans, which make little whimpers of pleasure escape.

Before I know what's happening, he has me on my hands and knees.

"You drive me crazy, Charlotte," he leans over me and whispers in my ear. "We're going to test this little voyeurism kink you have one day. I'm gonna take you somewhere we could easily get caught, and I'm gonna fuck you so hard you scream my name."

The idea of it has my body igniting. "Yes," I breathe.

"But for right now," he says as he pulls back and rubs his length around my clit. "I'm gonna enjoy taking you like this."

He slams into me with no restraint. I gasp at the shock of his invasion. Then he grabs my hair and pulls my head back.

"I've never taken a girl as rough as I wanted to. I always hold back," he growls while he remains seated in me, waiting for me to agree or tell him no.

"Fuck me exactly how you want to, Asher. Don't hold back," I tell him.

"Just tell me if it's too much," he warns. "Okay, baby?"

I meet his eyes and let him know I'm ready for whatever he wants to do to me. I doubt there's anything this man will do that won't feel incredible.

With his fist still in my hair, he tugs even harder. The pain in my scalp is intense but not unwelcome. It's sexy that he is filled with such desire for me that he can't contain himself. It makes me feel special. And the fact that he's never felt comfortable enough to do this with anyone else is something I'll be looking way too much into later—for sure.

This time, when he pulls out, he slams in so hard that he has to use his grip on my hair to keep me in place. The pain and pleasure mixed together is so intense. I do my best not to make too much noise, but there's no way in hell I can hold it all in. It's unlike anything I've experienced before.

His other hand grips my hip so hard that I know I'll have bruises there tomorrow. Then, I don't know how to explain what comes next. Just intense, hard, animalistic sex.

It's fast and demanding.

It's all-consuming.

It's the most pleasure anyone has ever pulled from my body, and I haven't even come.

I get lost in not only the pleasure but the sounds coming from him. He's clearly losing his mind, completely in his element. He's grunting, cussing, and moaning.

"Fuck, Charlotte. You look so damn sexy, letting me take you like this."

He repositions one of his legs so his left foot is planted flat on the mattress like he's on one bent knee. This allows him to get an angle slightly higher on top of me. When he drives forward and down, he hits directly on my G-spot.

"Oh, shit," I whisper.

"I'm gonna come so fucking hard inside of you. I want you to feel me for days."

With both of his hands on my hips, he thrusts into me over and over until we are both coming apart. Our orgasms seem to go on forever.

Once we're done riding out the waves of pleasure, he falls on top of me, forcing me to go face-first into the mattress.

I laugh at the shock of it all. Moving my head to the side so I can breathe.

His hot breaths are on my neck while our chests rise and fall in rapid succession.

"Sorry," he says as he rolls off me. "I think I blacked out there for a second."

He looks at me as I struggle to catch my breath, but I still manage a smile.

"Same." I suck in another breath. "Wow. That was…"

He rolls to his side to face me. "Yeah. It was…something. I didn't hurt you, did I?"

He gently tucks a stray hair behind my ear. The act makes my heart flutter.

"Only in the best possible way."

We both gaze into each other's eyes. I can tell he's thinking about something.

"What's on your mind?" I ask.

He sighs. "Lauren…I could never ask her for that." He pauses. "I don't mean to say anything bad about her or bring her up at such a weird time."

"I know. It's okay. I want you to tell me what's on your mind, and I'm glad you were able to tell me you wanted to do it. Really glad. Like…my vagina is eternally grateful."

He laughs, such a carefree laugh like he used to. It fills my heart with joy.

"Come on. Let's go rinse ourselves off," he says as he drags me out of his bed.

I put my hair up in a high ponytail and we spend the next ten minutes rinsing each other off in his tiny shower.

He lets me borrow a pair of his sweatpants and a shirt, then pulls me into his arms in his bed.

We fall into easy conversation, like it always seems to happen with us.

"You think your dad leaving you the house has any significance?" he asks once we start discussing the projects to work on.

I sigh. "Honestly, I try not to think about it. Ever since he left when I was seventeen, it's just been easier to avoid trying to understand his actions. I know it's not the healthiest way to handle it, but I don't really know what else to do."

His hand runs along my arm. It's so comforting. I feel like I could fall asleep.

"Now that he's gone, do you forgive him?"

It feels like this question holds a lot of weight for him. Does he have forgiveness he can't give out as well?

"I don't know the answer to that. There's still a lot of anger and resentment there. I guess I just don't understand his actions. He had to know he was hurting me. Why was it so easy for him to do it? You know?"

He lets out a breath. "Yeah, I know what you mean."

I raise an eyebrow at him. "Was there anything Lauren did that needs forgiveness?"

I feel his muscles go rigid. I can feel the anger radiating from him. "I don't really like to talk about it," he says coldly.

"Oh, okay. We can talk about something else."

"Sorry," he tells me. "It's just not something I like to rehash."

"No, I get it."

Luckily, we are able to move on and talk about other things for another hour before it's time for me to go back home.

I understand that we are still just getting to know each other, and his deceased wife is a heavy topic. But I hope he can open up to me about it one day. I'm beginning to sense that maybe Layla is right. Maybe he is holding onto something bigger than just her death.

Chapter Seventeen

Asher

"Doesn't look like a huge issue to me," Josh says as we examine the foundation of a massive house in Savannah. "Just some minor cracks in the foundation, but they don't point to a larger issue. We can have the guys fill them in and continue on with the work."

I walk through the basement with him, analyzing the cracks along the walls and the floor. Foundations are tricky, something you don't want to ignore. A small problem that isn't dealt with can become a major problem down the road.

"Yeah, I think you're right. Go ahead and tell them to fill them in and continue on with framing."

Josh nods his head in agreement. "You got it, boss."

"How many times have I told you to stop calling me that? You're my assistant in this. You manage just as much as I do."

"You're still the owner of the company. Which makes you my boss," he says, as he always does, when I point this out.

"I still don't like hearing it from you."

He chuckles as we walk back upstairs and outside toward my car. He throws down the latch of the tailgate and hops up on the bed of my truck.

"I'm surprised to see you here today," he admits as he grabs a cooler and pulls out a bottle of water.

"What do you mean? You always see me."

He looks at me pointedly. "Not lately. I think something else has been distracting you, or should I say...someone?"

"If you have something to say, just say it," I cut out sharply.

He throws his head back and laughs. "I talked to Bret the other day."

I roll my eyes. "Stop. Just stop. I don't need to hear about what you two girls were gossiping about. I have a pretty good idea."

"So, it is true," he says enthusiastically. "Hell yeah, man. Good for you."

"I never admitted to anything," I point out.

"So, you weren't making out with her on her deck?" He wiggles his eyebrows at me.

I punch him on his arm, and he feigns to be hurt, though I know I didn't hit him hard enough.

I chuckle to myself. "I didn't know he saw that part."

I suppose we were right there on the back deck, easily visible from the kitchen.

"Seriously, man. It's nice to see you like this," he says, patting my leg.

"Like what?"

"Smiling. Happy."

I grab my water bottle and take a big sip, not quite sure how to respond to that. I'm not great at discussing my emotions anymore. I'm out of practice. Once upon a time, talking about my feelings didn't scare me in the slightest.

"I just want to make sure, before you jump into this, that you've dealt with everything you need to. Charlotte seems like a catch, man, but she also appears independent and headstrong. She's not gonna put up with your bullshit if you lash out and refuse to open up."

He's right—I know he is—but I don't know what the hell I'm doing. I can't seem to stay away from her, and I'm crazy about her, but nothing has changed.

I don't see myself miraculously able to open up to someone and let them in again.

We sit in silence for a bit while my brain continues to spiral out of control.

"I'm not telling you to stop seeing her. You deserve to be happy," he says as he pats me on the shoulder.

"I know. I appreciate it."

"Don't freak out about it and overanalyze my words. Anyway, I should get back inside."

His words weigh on me while I drive home with Brie in the backseat after picking her up from my parents. The last thing I want to do is hurt Charlotte.

But she's also leaving at the end of the summer, so it's not like she can get hurt. She'd be the one leaving me.

Shit. My hands grip the steering wheel harder at the thought of her leaving.

If anything, I'll be the one nursing my wounds when she inevitably leaves. It's also not like she has any interest in becoming a stepmom.

I don't know what I'm worrying about. She is probably just looking for a summer fling while she's here. She said it herself: She's had a crush on me for years. It's probably just her fulfilling some teenage dream to get with her friend's older brother.

"Daddy!" Brie says in my arms as we're walking into the house.

"Yes, sweetie?" I ask as I kiss her chubby cheeks. I can't help it. They're my weakness.

"Beach, pwease?"

I put her down as soon as we walk through the door, and she turns up to look up at me.

"Beach!" she jumps up and down.

I chuckle at her enthusiasm. "We can't go to the beach right now. Maybe this weekend, if the weather is nice."

"Yay!" she jumps around all the way to the kitchen.

Thankfully, that was enough for her to feel content. I'm too tired to deal with a meltdown right now, though, and it's not like any parent has the energy for one.

"Do you want to help me make dinner?"

"I help!" she screams with excitement.

I pick her up and place her on the counter, then ask her to hand me the mini potatoes, and I start cutting them.

"What did you do with grandma and grandpa today?"

She holds a potato in her hand as she talks. "We bake! Apple pie, Daddy!"

"Apple pie. I love apple pie."

"Me too!" she says as she rubs her belly enthusiastically.

She's so darn adorable. I laugh as we continue to work together, loving this time we get together at the end of each day.

"Okay. Vegetables are cut. Let's throw these in the oven with the chicken."

I place her on the ground so she can watch me place it in the oven.

"What do you want to do while dinner cooks?"

"Color!"

"Coloring it is."

I get us set up at the kitchen table with paper and crayons.

"What should I draw?" I ask her.

I've learned that whatever I choose is a bad choice in her eyes, so it's best to just ask ahead of time.

"A house," she tells me. "And a pig!"

"A house and a pig it is. Got it. What are you going to draw?"

"Worry about yourself," she tells me.

I think my chin falls to the floor. "What did you just say to me? Where did you learn that?"

"Ganma. She says to Ganpa."

"Grandma says that to Grandpa?"

She shakes her head and sets about coloring on her page like nothing's wrong.

I'm officially stumped. If I tell her not to say that, am I throwing Grandma under the bus? But I have to correct her. I can't have her running around talking to people like that.

"Honey. That's not nice to say to anyone."

She looks at me like she's considering my words, deciding for herself whether or not she will choose to listen.

"Okay, Daddy," she says, then grabs a crayon and starts gliding it along her paper until she notices I'm still sitting here frozen. "Color, Daddy."

"Okay, sorry." I pick up my crayon and try my best to draw a house with a pink pig standing next to it. I'm not a very good artist, but I must admit I've gotten better.

Luckily, it passes the Brie test by the end, while I compliment her attempt at a horse. She's three, so it doesn't even look like an animal. Nonetheless, I try to make her feel special.

Once she's in bed for the night, I'm lying on the couch, and my brain keeps drifting to Charlotte. After my talk with Josh today, I know I should pump the breaks on this thing.

And yet, even as I say that to myself, I'm scrolling through my phone and calling her.

"Hey, you," her beautiful voice says through the speaker.

I smile instantly. "Hey, sexy. What are you doing?"

"Just took a shower. I did some more painting after work. My body is killing me. What about you?"

"I just got Brie in bed."

"How was your day?"

"It was good. Made some stops at the job sites to make sure everything was running smoothly. Brie and I colored when we got home, then had some dinner together."

A giggle rings through the phone. "I can't picture *you* coloring."

"I'm an excellent colorer," I say as I pretend to be offended.

"Is colorer even a word?"

I chuckle. "I don't think so. That's beside the point. My work is a hundred times better than Brie's," I joke.

She cracks up. "She's three, Asher."

How does she do this? Have me smiling on the phone like this?

Fuck it. I don't care if it's two nights in a row. I don't care if it's ten nights in a row. I want to see her.

"Do you, uh, have enough energy to drive over her again tonight?"

There's a silence for a second. "I have energy to do more than just drive over there."

A low growl releases from my lips. "Get over here now, babe."

She laughs. "I'll be there soon."

When she shows up not even ten minutes later, I have her against the wall in my living room within the first five seconds that I close the door.

I kiss her long and slow, not wanting to rush anything tonight. I walk her backward, keeping my hands on her hips until we make it to my bedroom.

Then I pull her shirt over her head while she gets rid of her shorts.

She's left in nothing but a red cotton bra and panty set. I lick my bottom lip while I let my eyes absorb her beauty.

"You're so beautiful, baby," I tell her.

She smiles softly at me. I grab my shirt from the neck and lift it off quickly, then start unbuttoning my jeans until I'm down to just my black boxer briefs.

Her eyes study my body unhurriedly. I stand still, letting her get her fill. It makes my dick even harder watching her admire me like this. She isn't shy about it, which is so damn sexy.

Then she steps closer and gently runs her fingers along my pecs. I try to reign in my breathing, but I've already lost control. That's the effect she has on me. I'm starting to think I've lost control of more than just my reaction to her touch, but I push that thought away.

"You are the beautiful one," she whispers. "I have a confession to make."

I stand still, wondering what it is she could want to admit right now. Worried it's something that will ruin the moment.

"What's that?"

"I used to have the biggest crush on you," she says shyly as she bites her lip.

I smile at her admission. "Did you now?"

I figured after her confession in her bathroom before she gave me the best blowjob of my life.

She nods her head. "Like, I wouldn't be able to think about anything but you for days after I saw you. It took months after summer vacation to try to get you off my mind. I knew I was just Layla's younger sister to you, and I was invisible to you."

I run the back of my finger up and down her cheek. "I wouldn't say invisible. I noticed your beauty from a distance. I mean, you were too young, so I never thought about you in that way."

"But you do now?" she smiles coyly.

I look down at my bulging cock. "What do you think?"

She smiles. "I could just worship your body all night."

She leans in and places a gentle kiss on my chest, which makes my body break out in a shiver.

"Aren't I supposed to say those things to you?"

"You do," she reminds me. "But I'm saying them to you."

Her fingers gently, slowly run down to my abs, where they move along the ridges of my stomach. She continues kissing my chest as her lips move closer to my nipples.

Ever so gently, she wraps her subtle lips around one of them and sucks.

"Fuck," I whisper as I watch on in shock.

No one has ever played with my nipples before. I didn't know it could feel so good.

She gently bites on one of them, which goes directly to my dick. That's about all I can handle before I pick her up over my shoulders. She squeals as I stomp over to the bed and throw her down.

She goes down laughing and giggling.

"You are such a dirty girl," I say as I fall down on top of her, grinding my pelvis into hers. "Do you feel what you to do me?"

I don't give her time to respond before I'm claiming her lips. While my tongue slowly mixes with hers, I reach down to her underwear and yank them down. She helps me out by kicking them off the rest of the way.

I start to push my boxers down while her foot helps me out and pushes them off.

I'm frantic, in desperate need of what only she can give me. I wrap my hand around my dick, give it one good tug and slide into her.

It's like everything else fades away when I'm inside of her. It's only the two of us, and nothing else seems to matter. It's both amazing and terrifying.

She wraps her legs around me and settles her feet on my back, urging me to start moving.

I kiss the tip of her nose, then her eyes, and finally her mouth, moving in and out of her unhurriedly.

As my hips push down, hers push up. We work together, creating a tempo that builds with every thrust.

Our bodies are so entwined together that I don't know where hers ends and mine begins. With our lips only a breath apart, our breathing becomes one. I didn't know it could feel like this, that two souls could come together so perfectly.

No words are spoken, just two people taking in the intensity of the moment as the pleasure mounts.

I feel her walls begin to grip me tighter, letting me know she's getting close. All the while, we keep our eyes locked on each other, not willing to break the connection between us.

I pick up the pace, driving in harder until she comes apart. I watch every detail of her beautiful face when she comes. The way her mouth falls open, her eyelids flutter, her moans fall from her lips.

It's mesmerizing.

My own release can't be held off any longer. With my forehead falling to her shoulders, I let myself go.

Chapter Eighteen

Charlotte

Two Weeks Later

"Avery," Layla shouts over the music. "Nobody wants to hear about how you stuck your finger up your boyfriend's butthole."

I nearly choke on my beer as I look around to make sure nobody heard that.

It's the Fourth of July celebration in Savannah on River Street. A live band is playing on a large stage set up near all of the food trucks and games.

We used to come here all the time with my parents. I love the energy.

I consider Avery's admission, maybe one she just made after one too many beers.

"Did he like it?" I find myself asking.

"He loved it," she says. "He came almost instantly."

"Hmm," I say. "Interesting."

Avery looks at me mischievously. "Are you going to try it on Asher?"

"Ewww!" Layla interrupts. "Just...no! Please, please. I beg of you. If you ever do such foul things to my brother, never, and I mean NEVER, tell me about it."

I throw my head back in laughter while Avery almost spits out her beer.

"I just asked a question," I defend.

"Auntie Layla!" a high-pitched little voice squeals from behind me.

I turn around and see the cutest little toddler running toward us. It dawns on me that she just spoke the words Auntie Layla which means—my eyes look behind her. My heart flutters in my chest when I see him walking behind her with the biggest smile on his face.

He watches with admiration as his daughter jumps into Layla's arms. Once she's safe in her auntie's arms, his eyes move to mine.

His eyes are brimmed with tenderness as he comes close to me, looking down on me intently.

"Hey, you," he says. "I didn't know you'd be here tonight."

I gaze up at his handsome face. "Layla was able to free herself from the café last minute." I look around at all the commotion. "I forgot how much I loved coming here for the Fourth."

Josh and Kyle show up behind Asher. Kyle goes right for Avery while Josh rolls his eyes at a scowling Layla.

"Who this?" Brie says in Layla's arms as her chubby little finger points in my direction.

I turn my attention to her and wave.

"Brie, this is my friend, Charlotte," Layla says. "We've known each other since we were kids."

"Hi. You pretty," she takes a piece of my dark hair and starts twirling it around her finger, "like my doll."

I try to suppress a giggle. "That's so sweet. Thank you. I love your dress." She's in the most adorable red, white, and blue dress with a matching bow in her hair. "Did your daddy pick this out?"

She chuckles. "No, silly. Ganma."

"You must have the best grandma," I tell her.

She smiles and shakes her head in agreement.

I notice a subtle look between Avery and Layla before Layla turns to me and Asher.

"Hey, we're going to go check out the band. Get a little closer. It's too crazy for Brie. Why don't you two take her to some of the games over there? Brie, do you want to go with Charlotte and Daddy to see the ducky game?"

"Yay!! Ducks. I wuv ducks!" she screams, then nearly jumps into Asher's arms.

Asher looks over at me. "You don't have to if you wanna stay with them."

"No, I'm happy to go with you guys. I love duckies too," I say to Brie, which makes her smile.

"Daddy. She wuvs duckies too!"

"No way. Looks like we better go see some duckies."

We weave in and out of crowds, me throwing my empty beer in a trash can along the way, until we get to a booth with a big water table filled with rubber ducks in an array of colors.

"It's duckies!" Brie shouts in Asher's arms.

She starts to turn her body around, looking to show me what she just discovered. I move up to the table and bend over.

"Look at all of these, Brie. There are so many colors," I say to her.

She wiggles her way out of Asher's arms until he puts her on the ground. She comes up to me and gets on her tippy toes, trying to see over the edge of the table. The table is eye level with her, making it hard for her to see.

She lifts her arms up at me. "Up, pwease."

I look down at her little arms stretched out to me like we're the best of friends. My heart swells. Leaning down, I hook my hands under her arms and lift her onto my hip.

"Which color is your favorite?" I ask her as we look at the rainbow of ducks floating by.

"Green!" she squeals.

I look over at Asher. "Got any money for us, Daddy?" I say as I wink at him.

He tries to act shocked at my question, but I see the smirk he's trying to fight as he pulls his wallet out. He hands the worker five dollars for us to pick up five ducks.

"Okay, sweetie. We get to pick up five ducks." I decide not to tell her that if there's a black marker line on the bottom, we win a prize.

It'll just be a nice little surprise for her if it happens.

"That one," she points to a green one floating by. "I want that one."

The worker picks it up and looks at it. No luck, but he hands her the duck, which makes her day.

"Quack, quack," she mimics with the duck.

I quack back at her, which makes her erupt in a fit of giggles. We pick another three ducks, which are all losers, but now Brie is juggling four rubber ducks and seems to be in heaven.

"Okay, last one," I tell her.

"You pick!" she tells me.

"Me? Okay...hmmm. I pick...that one." I point to a classic yellow duck.

"Winner!" the worker hollers after he flips the duck over.

Asher and I cheer at the same time while Brie looks between the two of us.

"You guys won," Asher says.

"We did it!" Brie cheers, even though she clearly has no clue what is going on.

A large teddy bear the size of Brie is handed to Asher while her face is in total awe.

"That mine?" she asks, her big blue eyes taking it all in.

"It's all yours," I tell her. She drops the ducks on the ground, old news to her, and reaches for the teddy bear.

Asher picks up the ducks and hands them back to the man working the booth. I think she is able to keep them, but I also don't think he's trying to carry five rubber ducks around the rest of the night.

"More games?" She looks at me.

"Of course, more games!" I reply.

Asher just shakes his head while I start to lead the way with Brie in my arms.

After a couple more games, during which we win glow-in-the-dark wands for the Fourth of July and some balloons, Brie and I stop to get our faces painted with red, white, and blue fireworks.

I snap a picture at the end of the two of us smiling into the camera. Tonight has been perfect. I'm having more fun than I've ever had at a festival, and it's all because of the company I have.

"I'm hungry," Brie says to Asher as soon as we walk away from the face-painting booth.

"Me too, sweetie," he replies, then looks to me. "Care to join us for some dinner? My treat."

I smile down at Brie, who's looking at me hopefully, then back at Asher. "I'd love to."

Ten minutes later, the three of us are sitting at a picnic table eating corn dogs on a stick. Brie is sitting on top of the table between us.

She has ketchup all over her face, but that seems to be the least of her worries.

"Yummy," she says in between a bite.

"I agree. Yummy," I reply.

Asher looks between the two of us, but I can't quite figure out what's on his mind. Every time his gaze meets mine, my heart turns over in response.

Asher has long been done with his corndog, so he leans over and takes a bite of Brie's.

"Daddy! Mine," she says as she tries to conceal her food.

My mouth falls open, feigning astonishment. "How dare you steal your daughter's food?"

"I'm hungry," he pouts.

"Well, you could at least wait to see if she finishes," I reply in Brie's defense.

"She's not gonna finish that corndog."

"You never know. She could've worked up an appetite after all of our..."

"I'm done," she cuts me off as she throws her dog back in her paper tray.

He looks over at me triumphantly. "You were saying," he mocks as he dramatically picks the leftover food off her tray.

Before he can take a bite, I lean in and take a big chomp off the dog myself.

"You were saying," I say to him with my mouthful.

Brie laughs hysterically. "She take big bite," she says with glee.

I raise my eyebrows at him while he still looks shocked.

"I can't believe you did that."

Brie is still in a fit of giggles, which makes Asher and me lose it. Before I know it, the three of us are cracking up together.

An elderly couple walks by, and the woman stops in front of us. "You three make a beautiful family," she says.

"Ooh, umm," I begin to say, but stumble over my words.

"Thank you," Asher cuts in.

Oh my god. He didn't correct her. He didn't freeze up in fear like I would've assumed. He just gladly took the compliment and let her go on with her day. It takes several minutes for my erratic heart to finally calm down.

We eventually finish our food as it starts to get dark.

Asher looks around at the crowd. "We should probably go find a good spot for the fireworks."

He puts Brie on his shoulders, and the two of us walk side by side to the grassy area with the best view of the fireworks show.

The entire time, my mind is stuck on the woman's comment about us being a family. It does feel natural right now, the three of us together.

But it's dangerous to have these thoughts. This was never discussed, me meeting his daughter. I don't want to let my heart fall for her, because I'm definitely already falling for her dad, which isn't part of the plan. I'm leaving soon.

"Here we go," Asher says as he finds a giant rock. He motions for me to take a seat then reaches for Brie, bringing her down to sit in between us.

We made it just in time for the fireworks to start. Brie has each of her little hands on one of our legs as she watches the sky in fascination.

"Wook at the colors," she says.

"They're beautiful," I reply. "I like the blue ones."

"Me too." She rests her head on my arm and yawns.

My heart melts into a puddle of love for her. I try to steal a glance at Asher without him catching me, but he is already watching us with tenderness in his eyes.

The moment is so perfect it's bringing tears to my eyes which I frantically try to blink away.

Once the grand finale approaches, the noise level increases, and Brie now has her hands over her ears.

"Too woud," she tells us.

Asher chuckles. "I think we should head back to the car anyway. It's way past her bedtime. I could take you home if you want. Unless you plan on meeting back up with the rest of the crowd."

"No, a ride home would be great. Thank you."

We walk back to the car while Brie is in Asher's arms resting her head on his shoulder. By the time we get to the car, she is passed out.

I can't resist rubbing her cheek as he places her in her car seat.

He comes around to open my door and helps me hop into his truck. I let him focus on maneuvering out of the crazy traffic while I keep peeking back at Brie. Her angelic face while she sleeps is precious, and I find that I can't get enough.

When we're finally on the road and out of traffic, I see Asher's shoulders relax.

"She's incredible," I whisper, not wanting to wake her.

He smiles. "She is."

"You're great with her."

His eyes look at me before focusing back on the road. "You are too. She loved you."

"I'm sure she loves everyone she meets."

He shrugs. "Not everyone who meets her hits it off like you two did."

We both sit in silence with those words hanging in the air.

When he pulls into my driveway, I want to ask him to stay, knowing he can't. I'm not ready to say goodbye tonight.

He leaves the car running. "I'll walk you to the door."

As soon as we approach the door, he gathers me into his arms and kisses me. I sink into his touch, parting my lips and arching my back to meet his kiss.

His lips move slowly and tenderly on mine. The faintest bit of tongue plays with mine, just enough to make my entire body shiver.

He pulls away and cups my cheeks.

"Goodnight, beautiful."

"Goodnight," I whisper.

Chapter Nineteen

Asher

"No Gandma and Ganpa today?" Brie asks in the back of my truck.

"Grandma isn't feeling well today. She has a cold," I tell her. "I just have a couple stops to make for work then we can spend the rest of the afternoon together."

She looks out the window, no complaints about being stuck with me today.

I carry her around on two of my job sites while I talk to some of the guys about some of the setbacks they are facing. As much as she wants to wiggle out of my arms, I can't let her run free on a construction site. Luckily, Josh just keeps talking while Brie plays with his hardhat that's still on his head. He's so good with Brie. We call him Uncle Josh because that's how I feel about our relationship. He's like a brother to me.

When I think we're done for the day, I get a text from Bret about coming to look at the final product at Charlotte's for approval. I instantly smile, excited that I get to see her.

As I walk up Charlotte's front porch with Brie in my arms, I start to get a bit nervous.

Will Charlotte think I'm overstepping by bringing my daughter to her house?

I take a deep breath. I'm dancing around dangerous territory here—territory I told myself I would never be in again. Now, it's not just my heart on the line—it's Brie's.

I knock on the door before I can talk myself out of this. Charlotte opens it within seconds. She must've been standing right by the front.

Her face instantly lights up when she sees Brie in my arms.

"Hi, Brie." She opens up her arms, and Brie leans forward in a trust fall right into her arms.

Brie gives her cheek a kiss. My heart can't handle the sight. I look down at my boots to try and stop these emotions that are tearing down barriers I thought I built firmly around my heart.

"What are you two doing here?" she asks with delight.

I step inside and follow her to her kitchen table.

"Bret called and asked for the final inspection now that everything is done."

"It's incredible, isn't it? They did such a good job. With the painting and the floors done, it's like a new house."

I look around at the floors, noticing how they don't look worn anymore. The color is dark and rich, popping off the lighter colors on the walls. Charlotte also painted all of the golden oak trim white, which helps the floors stand out even more. The place does look so much better. I'm so proud of Charlotte for taking all of this on by herself. She's something else.

"Care if I walk around and take a look so I can tell Bret if I notice any areas that need work?"

"No, go for it. Brie and I will just hang out while you do that. Is it okay if I walk outside with her and show her the view?"

"That's fine. I'll come find you guys when I'm done."

It only takes me about fifteen minutes to inspect everything to determine that it looks good. It always does with my guys. I only hire the best.

I walk outside onto the deck to find the two off in the distance sitting on the dock by the water watching the boats go by.

I always grew up on the water, it's part of who I am. I have a boat stored by a marina not far from here that I haven't had time to take out since the beginning of summer. Life has just been so crazy, and I've also spent all of my free time with the beautiful woman who's stealing my heart.

But growing up, my dad and I would always go fishing together. I remember passing by this house all the time, seeing a young Layla, Charlotte, and Avery waving at us from this very dock.

Who would've thought this was where life was going to lead us?

I reach the end of the dock, hands in my pockets as I watch them.

"Dolphins?" Brie asks softly.

"Yes, dolphins. I saw a few this morning. That's why I bought these chairs to put out here, it's one of my favorite places."

"I wuv dolphins."

"Me too. They're my favorite. Growing up, I used to beg my dad to let me jump in the water and swim with them."

"You swim wif dolphins?"

"Sadly, no. You're not allowed to swim with wild dolphins. But it never stopped me from coming out here and watching them, wishing they could be my friends."

"I be your friend," Brie says then gives Charlotte a hug.

"I would love that. Thank you, sweetie pie."

"I'm all finished," I interrupt, not sure I can handle hearing any more of this without losing another piece of the protective armor around my heart.

"Daddy! Dolphins in the water," Brie says, still sitting in Charlotte's lap on the chair.

I take a seat in the spare chair next to them.

"There are dolphins in this water," I reply, agreeing with her statement.

"We go to the beach?" she asks.

"This weekend we're going to the beach."

"Yay!" You come?" Brie turns to Charlotte.

"Oh, um, I think your daddy might not want..." Charlotte stumbles on her words.

I know I shouldn't push this, all of us spending time with together, but I can't help myself.

"You should come. If you're free, and if you'd like to."

She smiles at me. "I'd love to come."

We sit in silence for a while, looking out at the water. A big fishing boat rolls by, which catches our attention.

"I haven't been on a boat in forever," Charlotte says, breaking the silence.

I look over at her and see her admire the boats that go by.

"I have a boat. I was thinking about taking it out this weekend. You wanna come with me?"

"Seriously? You have a boat?" she exclaims.

"I do."

"When are you thinking of taking it out?"

"Layla was going to take Brie for the night after our beach day. I was going to do an evening cruise, maybe try to catch some fish."

"I'd love to join you."

"It's a date." I smile at her, then glance back at the water.

"Daddy, I'm hungry."

"Yeah, we need to head home anyway so I can start dinner."

"Charwotte come too?" Brie asks.

I look at her sympathetically. "I'm sure Charlotte has things to do, sweetie."

Brie looks up at her with big doe eyes. "You don't wanna come?"

"Oh, um, of course I would. I don't know if your daddy really wants..." Charlotte begins, but Brie is already jumping off her lap in excitement.

We both lunge for her to make sure she doesn't fall into the water. When I pick her up into my arms and rest her on my hip, Charlotte puts her hand on her heart.

"Come on, let's go." Brie motions us along.

"You don't have to come. She's actually not in control, as much as she thinks she is sometimes."

Charlotte shrugs her shoulders. "I don't mind if you don't mind."

Do I mind? Of course, I would love the company. And Brie is obviously enamored with her. There is still the nagging thought in the back of my mind telling me to be careful.

"I don't mind," I tell her, deciding it's just dinner. "I'd actually love the company."

"Okay, well, I'll meet you guys there. I just need to send out a couple more emails."

At the end of the dock, we walk our separate ways and agree to meet at my house.

I'm nervous as hell. I can't remember the state of my house, but I'm sure it's not clean enough. It's not like she's going to walk in and start checking for dust, but I can't remember the last time I actually did dust.

Once we're home, I set Brie up with a small snack while I run around the house picking things up. Blocks are everywhere on the ground, crayons on the kitchen table with paper scattered about.

A pile of half-folded laundry sits on the couch in the family room. I place it all into a laundry basket, hoping to keep the piles somewhat organized so all work isn't lost.

I start to run toward the kitchen to put dirty dishes in the dishwasher, but somehow miss the baby doll on the floor. My foot gets stuck in between the legs of the doll, and I go flying toward the end table next to the couch.

It feels like it's all happening in slow motion. I can see the table inching closer to my face, but I can't seem to dodge it.

It smashes into my forehead, and I bounce off the damn table like a ping-pong ball.

I groan on the floor as the pain radiates through my head.

"Shit," I whisper to myself.

"Daddy!" Brie hops off her booster seat and joins me on the floor. "You okay?"

I let out another groan. "I'm okay," I croak just as the doorbell rings.

Shit. She's here. I roll over and slowly pick myself up off the ground before I stumble to the front door, holding my head.

I open the door and hear a loud gasp come from Charlotte. "Oh my god. You're bleeding."

I pull my hand away from my head, and sure enough, there's blood all over it.

She walks into my house without a second thought and grabs my hand. She leads me to my couch, where she helps me sit.

"Here." She lightly touches my face. "Lie your head back. I'm gonna go get something to clean you up."

"Daddy hit his head," Brie says as she follows Charlotte.

I can't quite make our what they say to each other after they leave the room. I just know my head hurts, and I'm embarrassed as fuck.

The couch next to me dips, and I open my eyes. Charlotte wipes up some blood with a paper towel, then presses a warm washcloth to my forehead.

"Okay, let's hold this here for a minute."

I stare into her beautiful green eyes and feel my body begin to relax. My blinding pain begins to settle into intense throbbing.

"Thank you," I whisper, her scent permeating the air around me.

Brie climbs up into my lap. "You okay, Daddy?" she asks lightly.

I reach for her and rub her back. "I'm better now, sweetie. I just need a minute and I'll cook us dinner."

"Absolutely not." Charlotte pulls the washcloth from my face. "I'm going to order us something to eat. You need to rest."

"No, no," I say as I move Brie to the couch and try to stand up, but the pounding just gets worse.

She pulls me back to the couch. "Stop being so stubborn and let me order us some food."

I want to fight her on it, but I know I'm in no condition to cook, so I give in. She puts in a call for pizza while I lie down on the couch and put on a movie for Brie. Charlotte makes me take some medicine before I let myself rest.

Brie snuggles up next to Charlotte on the loveseat.

"Don't go falling asleep over there," Charlotte warns. "We need to make sure you don't have a concussion. If you start drifting off, I'm going to have to make you sit back up."

"I'm just going to rest for a bit. I promise."

I close my eyes to try to let the throbbing settle. For thirty minutes straight until the pizza arrives, Charlotte asks me every couple of minutes if I'm awake. I think it's a little overkill, but don't have the heart to tell her she's overreacting.

The medicine and rest helped a little. It just feels slightly sore and only hurts a little bit.

I sit up slowly to see if the pain gets worse, then I walk to the kitchen, where Charlotte is putting Brie into her booster seat.

"You don't have to get up. I can bring a slice to you."

"No, I'm good. I just need to take it easy, but I think it's safe to say there's no concussion. Just a minor headache and a whole lot of embarrassment."

I take a seat and Charlotte puts two slices in front of me then gives us each some salad.

"Nothing to be embarrassed about. I'm just happy I'm here to help." She takes a bite of pizza. "How exactly did it happen?"

"I, uh, tripped," I answer vaguely.

"I figured that much. Where did you hit your head?"

"On the end table by the couch."

She winces. "That doesn't sound good. What did you trip over?"

I grunt. "A baby doll."

She giggles over her pizza. "I'm sorry. It's not funny," she says but continues to laugh. "I just didn't expect a baby doll to take a big man like you down."

"Let's never talk about this again."

She just cracks up more, which makes Brie erupt into a fit of giggles. I start to laugh myself as I picture what I must've looked like getting taken down like that.

Charlotte now has tears running down her cheeks.

The laughing starts to make my head hurt. I grab my head and wince.

"What's wrong?" Charlotte stops laughing immediately. "Are you okay?"

"Yeah. I'm fine. I guess laughing doesn't agree with my head right now."

"Noted. From here on out, no laughing."

After we finish our dinner, Charlotte insists on being the one to give Brie her bath. I sit on the toilet while she is on her knees washing Brie's hair.

It's surreal to watch the two of them doing such a mother/daughter thing together. Charlotte is so natural with Brie. I can almost picture this being a regular occurrence for us, which is terrifying.

When she's done, Charlotte scoops her up and wraps her up in her pink unicorn towel, completely unaware or unaffected by the fact that she is getting wet.

She places her on the counter and grabs the brush that is sitting on a tray. She brushes Brie's hair while the two of them laugh and talk. I don't know that I can deny my feelings any longer to myself.

I'm in love with Charlotte.

I don't know how she did it. I thought I had a steal cage around my heart. As scary as it is, it also feels good.

I feel lighter and happier these days. I'm just scared because that's how you set yourself up to get hurt.

Chapter Twenty

Charlotte

"Did you really think that I'd be able to come see you and just eat lunch?" he says in between my legs.

I'm too far gone to even register what the hell he is saying. All I know is that I'm seconds away from coming, and I'm seeing stars.

"I could eat this pussy every day of my life. It's all I've been thinking about doing since last night."

I register what he's saying as I try to hold out longer.

"You. Just. Did. This. Last. Night," I breathe out.

"I know. I missed it the second I was done." He flicks his tongue roughly against my clit while he moans. "Come for me, baby. Come all over my mouth. I want to feel those juices leaking out onto my face."

Shit. Those dirty words do me in, and I obey his command.

It doesn't take long for him to move up my body and slide his dick into me. It's the best lunch break I've ever had.

After we finish, he's holding me and his hand runs a path up and down my arm. It's the most content I've ever felt.

Being with him makes me feel complete.

"How's your head doing?" I ask as I see the cut with a big lump around it.

"It's fine. Doesn't really hurt anymore. Josh got it out of me today, how I fell. I don't think he's laughed that hard in a long time."

My body rocks with laughter. "Somehow, I doubt that. Josh seems to laugh at everything."

He smiles. "Alright, I might be exaggerating."

"Thanks for helping with Brie the other night. It would've been a hell of a night trying to push through that headache without you."

"It was my pleasure. I loved every second of it."

"You did, huh?" he asks thoughtfully.

"You two have an amazing little life together, Asher. You're clearly an incredible father."

He sighs. "It doesn't always feel like it. I don't know what I'm doing half the time."

"I'm clearly no parenting expert, but I doubt anyone knows what they're doing half the time. I can tell you from the outside looking in, you're doing great."

He lifts up to his elbow and looks down at me. "Thank you," he whispers as he peers at me intently. Then he brushes a gentle kiss across my lips.

"What do you say we take a shower?" he suggests with his lips over mine.

"Good idea," I whisper into him.

We both get out of bed. I head for the shower to start it so the water can warm up.

"Can you grab some towels in the closet?" I shout to him.

As I walk back into the bedroom, I see he opened the single closet door instead of the large master closet.

"Oh, it's not that one," I say as he stands in front of an empty closet.

Empty except for the large cardboard box sitting on the floor.

"What's that?" he asks.

"I don't know. I haven't even opened this door since I've been here." I peer inside to see frames stacked on top of each other.

I slide the box out, curiosity getting the best of me.

"It's pictures...of my family."

I pick up the first frame. It's a picture of my parents and me sitting on our back deck together. The three of us are smushed together in the frame, smiling brightly at the camera.

It looks like I was about fifteen at the time.

A tear slips from my eye as I look at a time of my life that was so much simpler. You can see it in my carefree smile.

I place the frame next to me and grab the next one. As I pick them up, I realize they are all pictures of me and my mom. The bottom of the box is piles and piles of individual family photos.

All discarded and shoved in the back of a closet for an entire decade.

My sadness morphs into anger. I just picture my father grabbing all the frames around the house and tossing them into this box like we meant nothing to him.

Then I picture Penelope asking him what to do with it as they pack up the house.

"Just throw it in the closet. I don't want those," he says, indifferent to the memories these pictures hold.

I grab the picture frame off the ground and slam it back into the box. The glass shatters into a million pieces, much like my heart feels.

I grab two towels and storm off into the bathroom. Tears stream down my cheeks as my body begins to shake from the furry, from the pain.

"Charlotte," Asher whispers as he places his hands on my arms. "Come here."

He spins me around and forces me to look up at him. Hands on my neck, he tries to dry my tears with his thumbs, but they are coming too quickly.

"Sweetheart, talk to me."

The concern in his voice only makes my tears come faster.

"Why didn't he want me?" I cry, my body feeling weak.

He wraps an arm around my waist to hold me up. "Who? Your father? Why would you say that he didn't want you?"

Asher opens the shower door and lifts me up as he walks us into it. Once he places me back down, he waits for my answer.

"He left me. He moved on with a new family. He never came back to see me, never tried to call me. I was just some expendable daughter who just made his life more complicated than he thought it was worth. And now…" my voice quivers as I look down. I try to take a breath and then look back up at him. "Now I find all his memories of me tossed aside in a closet. Forgotten. Just like he forgot me."

Admitting that out loud brings a relentless flow of tears that portray the width of my despair. My body begins to shudder as I let out the many years of pain I've spent without the man who was supposed to protect me.

Asher wraps his arms around me and begins to make soothing sounds. He doesn't press me to talk or try to make me feel better. He just holds me as I let it all out.

When no more tears can come, and my body feels spent, he lets go of me.

"No father should ever make their daughter feel like this. You are amazing. He's an idiot for losing out on all those years with you. I'm sure it was his biggest regret."

"What if it wasn't? What if he didn't miss me at all?"

He shakes his head. "Impossible. I don't know his reasons, none of which are good enough, but I can tell you there is no way he didn't miss you."

"You think so?"

"I know so. Trust me."

I don't know whether he means what he says or if he's just trying to cheer me up, but it's working.

"Thanks." I step back and take a deep breath. "Gosh, I'm so sorry. I'm so humiliated that you saw this."

"I'm honored that you felt safe enough with me to show me your pain." He reaches for the shampoo on the shelf. "Now, turn around and let me pamper you."

My body is drained from all the emotions I just brought to the surface.

I nod my head in agreement and turn around.

Asher pours the shampoo into his hand and nudges me under the water.

"Head back, baby," he whispers.

I let my head fall back into the steady stream of water. My eyes close as I enjoy the feeling of the warm water hitting me.

After my hair is wet, I lift my head.

He starts to lather my hair with the shampoo, then slowly massages my scalp with his expert touch. It instantly draws a moan out of me.

He spends the rest of our shower spoiling me with more scalp massages and even massages my body.

I tried not to get aroused, but it was impossible.

So, he took me against the shower wall, where I came apart in his arms.

Now we're dressed and walking downstairs. I hate that we both have to get back to work.

When we get to the front door, he turns around. His lips press against mine as they gently cover my mouth.

We take our time with each other. His lips tenderly move along mine.

"How about you come over for dinner tonight? I promise I won't hurt myself and cook this time."

I chuckle at the memory. "Sounds great."

He gives me one last kiss. "See you tonight, babe."

Chapter Twenty-One

Asher

"Brie, do you wanna build a sandcastle with me?" Charlotte asks after we take a break from the water.

"Yay!" Brie exclaims as she runs toward her sand tools. "Shovel!" she shouts, holding her big orange shovel.

I start to pick up the sand toys, but Charlotte stops me.

"I got this," she tells me. "Why don't you just relax."

"Relax?" I ask.

"Yes, relax. It's when you sit or lie down and do nothing."

"I haven't relaxed in three years."

"Well," she reaches for the toys. "It looks like today is your lucky day."

Charlotte turns around. "You ready, girlie?"

The two walk next to each other until they are closer to the water, where Charlotte finds a spot for them to take a seat.

I wasn't kidding when I told her I don't relax. I haven't had any time to myself for three years. Even if my parents are watching Brie for me to go out, it's because somebody is dragging me out of the house, and that's not exactly relaxing.

Lying down and doing nothing has become a foreign concept to me.

I reapply some more sunscreen, then move my towel out of the umbrella to the open sand. Relaxing in the warmth of the sun has always been soothing to me.

As soon as I lie back and close my eyes, my brain conjures up an image of Charlotte in her red bikini.

I've had to be on my best behavior today since Brie is with us. But it's taken herculean effort to keep my hands off her.

It's torture to be around a woman I'm completely crazy for while she prances around in a two-piece bathing suit.

Eventually, I'm able to focus on the feeling of the sun on my skin. My brain calms down, and my muscles even decompress.

It's exactly what I needed. I only relaxed for fifteen minutes, not wanting to take advantage of Charlotte's time, but it was fifteen minutes of peace and quiet.

I want to reapply Brie's sunscreen anyway, so I grab the bottle and head down to meet them at their spot.

Both girls look up at me with big smiles on their faces. My heart aches from the amount of love it generates.

"I thought I told you to relax," Charlotte says as I sit down.

"I did," I tell her. I open the sunscreen and start to apply it to Brie while she continues to dig. "I relaxed for fifteen minutes. It was incredible and exactly what I needed. But now I want to spend the rest of the time we have left with my girls."

Charlotte bites her lip. I wonder if she's trying to hide her reaction to me calling them my girls.

Either way, she's fucking adorable trying to hide her grin.

"Daddy, look." Brie points to her hole. "It's a baby pool."

"It's an awesome baby pool." I look around at the piles of sand. "I thought you were going to build a sandcastle."

Brie giggles. "I stomp on it."

Charlotte and I both busted out in laughter.

"We switched to digging holes," Charlotte says cheerily.

Once it hits three, I know we need to get back to drop Brie off at Layla's. Charlotte wanted to be dropped off first so she could rinse off.

It only takes me about thirty minutes total to drop off Brie and then get back to Charlotte's. Before I get up her porch steps, she comes out in a black casual dress that cuts above her knees.

Her hair is down in some beachy-looking waves.

My stomach tightens just looking at her.

She holds up a bottle of wine.

"I figured we could have a little fun while on the boat."

We walk our way back to my truck.

"I can have one glass's worth of fun since I'll be driving the boat," I tell her as I open the door and help her in.

"I guess I'll be having a lot of fun on my own tonight," she says as she raises her eyebrows at me.

I close the door and shake my head as images of her having fun on her own in a different way float through my head.

I start the truck, and we head toward the marina. My hand reaches for her thigh, resting on her soft skin as we listen to the music.

It takes about fifteen minutes, but as I park, I realize we didn't say anything to each other the entire ride. But it wasn't weird. It was comfortable—nice even.

I decided against fishing tonight. I don't want to focus on anything other than Charlotte.

After I help her out of the truck, I grab the bag I packed for us out of the truck bed. We walk along the dock, down the row of boats, until we reach mine.

"Here we are," I say as I stop in front of it.

I place my bag and her bottle of wine over the edge onto one of the seats, and then I hop down onto the boat first.

She reaches her hands toward me. I place them on my shoulders and grab her hips to pull her over.

"I can't believe this is your boat. It's incredible. I wasn't picturing a speed boat."

I move along the boat, getting everything ready while Charlotte sits on one of the seats.

"Can I do anything?" she asks.

"Do you know anything about boats?" I ask.

She chuckles. "I'm an Ohio girl. I don't know anything other than I love watching them and being on them."

"You're such a mid-western girl."

"What the hell is that supposed to mean?"

I smile, then lean down and give her a kiss. "It's cute."

"Saying it's cute doesn't make that comment any less annoying," she says as she stands.

Before she can get another word out, I place my hand on the small of her back and pull her body against mine, claiming her mouth.

I move my lips along hers, tasting her vanilla lip gloss that has made her lips perfect for kissing. Our lips slide against each other's, and I groan when she pushes her hips into me.

I pull her away from me, not meaning to feel so affected by our kiss.

"Does that make it less annoying?" I ask breathlessly.

She smiles. "That's cheating."

I shrug my shoulder. "I never claimed to be a gentleman."

The look in her eyes tells me she's thinking something right now that could get us both in trouble.

"Keep looking at me like that, and we'll have another repeat like the other night. I'll take you as rough as I can right here. No matter who's watching."

I reach for the rope and pull it off the dock then take a seat and turn the key. The boat fires up, and my body instantly starts to feel free of stress.

This has been my happy place since Lauren died. I bought it six months after she passed. The only one who's ever been on it with me is Brie—until today.

My family keeps giving me shit about it, but it's been the one place I can go to quiet my brain. Without it, I don't think I would've survived.

I didn't want it to become a loud party boat and ruin it for me.

The sun is slowly making its way down. I think we have about ninety minutes until it's dark.

It's the perfect time to take Charlotte out.

Once I have the boat pulled out and we are wading through the water, I take a second to steal a glance at her in the seat at the front of the boat.

She is facing the water, her back toward me, but it's the best view I've ever had on this boat. The sun is painted with pinks and oranges behind her, the perfect backdrop for the star of the scene—Charlotte.

She turns around with a big smile on her face.

"It's beautiful," she says. "Just...breathtaking."

"I agree," I tell her, not talking about the water or the sky.

We're just about out of the wading zone.

"You ready to fly, baby?" I ask.

"Are you kidding me? I'm born ready," she says, then throws her head back laughing as I push the lever forward.

We start to pick up speed instantly.

She laughs and screams as I take the boat to the edge of the water then cut the steering wheel to go back in.

We keep it up for a while, enjoying the wind against our skin, through our hair, forgetting that we're both older now. That life has fucked us both.

After seeing her broken and crumbled in front of me the other day, I knew I would do anything for her.

It gutted me. The worst was knowing there wasn't a damn thing I could do to take away her pain.

Once we get to the part of the water where I know my anchor can reach, I slow the boat to a stop.

I throw the anchor down until I feel the vibrations of it hitting the ground.

"Is it time for some wine?" she asks excitedly.

"Absolutely. And I also have a little something for dessert."

I pull it out of my bag, along with the fork I packed.

"Ooh, what is it?"

I take a seat on the back of the boat, where the long row of seating is, then motion for her to sit in between my legs.

"It's my mom's special peach pie."

"Shut the hell up! I haven't had your mom's pie in ten years."

She sits in between my legs, then leans her back against me in the crook of my arm.

"I forgot you've had this before."

"It's my favorite."

I pull the lid off the container and grab the fork. I push a little sliver of the pie on the fork.

"Open wide," I say.

She follows my instructions and opens without hesitation.

A moan falls from her lips as her head falls back into my arm. "It's heaven. Absolute heaven."

I take a bite for myself. "She knows how to make a mean peach pie."

We alternate bites as she leans into me, enjoying the sunset. It's something I would've loved to do with Lauren, but I picture her telling me it was too muggy out or her hair would get messed up.

She would definitely tell me peach pie has too many calories.

I place the empty container on the floor and then wrap my arms around her.

Kissing the side of her forehead, I watch the colors continue to fade away, replaced by darkness. We talk for a while, about my parents, about her mom. What they've been up to all these years.

I tell her about my parents' retirement.

She tells me she doesn't know when her mom can retire. Since she spent most of her childhood being the caretaker, her mom didn't have a retirement plan and didn't get any of her father's in the divorce settlement.

She tells me she will never allow herself to be financially dependent on anyone.

I respect the hell out of her for it.

Knowing it's going to take us at least thirty minutes to get back to the marina, I figure we should leave now.

Once I pull the anchor up, I sit down and turn the boat around.

With the sun now gone, it's a bit cooler when the breeze hits you. I notice Charlotte shivering and nod for her to join me.

I motion for her to sit on the edge of the seat, between my legs then wrap my body around hers while I drive.

Her head rests next to mine.

I knew bringing her on my boat was the right decision. She just adds to the peaceful tranquility I feel on here.

She adds it to my life every second that I'm with her.

Once we're wading through the water, on our way back to the dock, it's peaceful and dark.

"Thanks for bringing me out here," she says to me as she starts to pick up.

"Thanks for coming."

"And to think I almost went out with Avery, Josh, and Paul. I'm glad you asked."

I clench my mouth tight. "What are you talking about?"

"Nothing," she says coolly. "Avery just invited me to dinner. She said Josh and Paul were gonna be there."

"Like...a date?" I ask, my mouth set in annoyance.

"No, not like a date. Just friends going out to dinner."

"I don't like you going out to dinner with Paul."

I do my best to park the boat despite the emotions raging through me. As soon as it's parked, I grab the rope and loop it around the dock.

"Not just with Paul."

"Yeah, you and Paul with another couple. Sounds like a date to me."

It's happening again. I knew letting down my walls was going to kick me in the ass. Here she is, already showing warning signs of someone who is careless with another's heart.

I should heed the warning and walk away from it all right now.

"It's not like that," she defends as I help her back onto the dock.

"Excuse me for not believing a damn thing you say when you were about to go on a double date without telling me."

As soon as I know she's got her balance, I storm off toward my truck. I toss the bags in the bed and get into the front, starting the truck immediately.

She lets herself in, and we sit in silence for a minute as I drive.

This time, the silence is deafening. There's no comfort to it.

"Care to tell me what is going on?" Charlotte asks, breaking the silence.

I grip the steering wheel. "I really shouldn't have to spell it out for you."

She replies, voice hoarse with frustration, "Well, I'm not getting it, so you're going to have to spell it out for me."

We pull into her driveway, and I slam the truck into park.

"Okay!" I shout. "You want me to spell it out for you? I don't trust *anyone*. And when I hear the woman I'm spending all my time with is going on a double date, I'm bound to get a little angry! Because you going to a dinner with a couple and one other man, who might I add, has shown interest in you, that's called a double date. It's not that fucking difficult to understand."

"Don't talk to me like that. I didn't do anything wrong. Even if it was Paul's intention to view it as a double date, it doesn't mean it was mine. Maybe you need to figure out why you don't trust anyone."

"I know why I don't trust anybody. And don't try to be a therapist to me and ask me why. Trust me, I have good reason."

"And the reason is?"

"It's none of your damn business."

"Fine!" she screams as she opens the door. "If it's none of my business, then I guess we're done here."

I'm hot on her heels, not giving her a chance to get away from me.

"Now you're just going to walk away from me?" I yell, pounding up the steps behind her.

She turns around, walking backward. "What's the point? You're just going to assume I'm some kind of two-timing woman without even telling me why."

A tear slips down her cheek, gutting me on the inside. I don't want to do this to her. I hate my issues coming between us.

"I just want to know you," she whispers.

Her back hits her door. I walk in between her legs. My forehead falls to hers, closing my eyes.

"You do know me," I tell her, voice fragile and shaky. "You know my heart. There are just some things that hit a certain button of mine."

What I should be doing is re-evaluating if what we're doing is a good idea, but I find myself too desperate for her to do the right thing.

My mouth claims hers in a frantic kiss.

"We should talk about this," she says with my mouth still on hers.

"I know," I agree, then twist the doorknob as we tumble inside.

Her arms wrap around my neck as our kiss becomes demanding. My anger is still present, still blazing through me.

We fumble around, then end up backed against the island. My lips are punishing on hers, letting her know that I'm still reeling with jealousy.

I pull my lips away from hers, grab her dress, and pull it over her. My hands grip her face, and I smash my lips back down on hers.

"Take me like you did the other night," she breathes into my mouth. "I want it to hurt."

I growl at her request.

If she wants it rough, I have plenty of emotions in me to give her just that. I flip her around and push her forward onto the island.

Then I grab her panties and rip them off her, reveling in the scream she gives me.

"You want me to shove my cock so far up your pussy that you'll feel me for days?" I ask while my fingers glide through her glistening folds.

"Yes! Please!" she begs.

Hearing her beg for it is all that I can take. I unzip my shorts and pull my dick out, then I push inside of her so fiercely we both cry out at the sensation.

I take her exactly how she asked. Rough, hard, and fast. I choose to forget about the fight or the dark cloud hanging over the month we have until she leaves me.

Chapter Twenty-Two

Charlotte

I know I should be working, but my brain is replaying the events of Saturday over and over again. The sex was amazing. It was passionate and intense, a level of intimacy I'd never experienced before in my life. Until Saturday, I thought those books that portrayed sex as some kind of mystical connection between two people as some fantasy world that doesn't exist.

As magical as it was, we never actually talked about the fight afterward. He seems to want to ignore the entire thing.

I think it's because he doesn't want to tell me what had him so worked up. He doesn't want to tell me why he can no longer trust anyone.

Part of me wants to push him on it, but another part is terrified to. I don't want what we have to end right now, and I can see him walking away if I push too hard.

Though, we haven't talked about what happens when I go home in four weeks. The end of summer is getting closer. With each day that passes, the pressure to have a discussion with Asher about us grows stronger.

The doorbell rings, pulling me out of my glum train of thought. The only person who stops by without notice is Asher.

When I open the door, a delivery man is standing there with a large envelope tucked under his arm.

"Are you Charlotte Bates?" the gentleman asks.

"I am."

"Sign here, please," he says as he hands me a clipboard. "This is an overnight delivery from Howard Hart."

That's my father's attorney. I sign the pad in front of me and then take the envelope. "Thank you," I tell him before I close the door.

It's probably some additional papers regarding the house.

I tear open the envelope to see a handwritten note on a yellow piece of paper.

Charlotte,

I was going through your father's files and came across this letter he wrote to you. I'm terribly sorry that it got lost in the mix.

Sincerely,

Howard Hart

My trembling hand reaches inside to find a smaller white envelope. My name is written in cursive on the front in my father's handwriting.

I don't know if I have the courage to read his words.

Since it's lunchtime, I shut my laptop and walk outside onto the deck. My nerves are so active that they feel tingly all over my body. If I'm going to read this, I at least need to be in my happy place.

I take a seat on the cushioned couch and fold my legs underneath each other.

Then I open the envelope and unfold the papers, which are handwritten as well. Just seeing his handwriting like this makes my chest fill with overwhelming emotions.

Charlotte,

If you're reading this, I can only assume I'm gone, and we've never had a chance to reconnect.

As I sit here in my office thinking about what to say, I'm transported back to when you were little, as I often find myself thinking about.

I think about the first time you walked into my arms. The feeling that is evoked was pure pride and joy. Feeling the warmth of your love wrapped around me was the most content I've ever felt.

There were many firsts I got to experience of yours throughout your life, each one made my heart feel so full.

But the sad truth is, there were many firsts that I missed out on. From graduating college to your first job, your first apartment, first love.

I watched from afar, looking at your social media pages.

I was never not there with you, following in your successes along the way.

But I am a weak man. I didn't know how to be a husband to Penelope and a father to you.

Penelope was never trying to be intentionally evasive about our relationship, but she never did try to make it a priority in our new family. That was my fault for not having enough courage to stand up for our relationship. I suppose there might also have been some worry on her part. Worry that if you and I were close, you would somehow convince me to go back to your mother.

I tried to calm her nerves about it, but it never worked. Eventually, I pulled away, not knowing how to blend my two worlds.

It was wrong. It was selfish. It was unfair to you, and it is my biggest regret.

I'm not trying to make any excuses for my actions over the years. When I left your mother, I was not in a good place.

I did all that I could to ignore facing my demons.

You were the innocent one who faced the consequences of my poor decisions in life.

I'm hoping that you can find it in your heart to forgive me.

I know I don't deserve it, but if you do, it will be a gift that you did not need to grant me.

But I would like to find a place in your heart again. One where you can think of our times together and smile. Because those times were the best times of my life, and I would give anything to go back to those days. To right my wrongs. To be a better, stronger man.

If there's one thing I can leave you with, it's to know that my love for you never wavered.

I love you fiercely. You will always be my greatest accomplishment in my lifetime.

Love you always and forever,

-Dad

I put the letter down as I choke through my sobs of heartache.

All these years, I thought he had moved on without a care in the world. All these years I spent *hating* him.

I'm still angry at him for staying away, for leaving me behind. I don't know that you can ever completely lose the anger. Or maybe, over time, with these words, the anger will subside.

Knowing that he didn't want it to be like this hurts, but it also makes it better. If we both wanted to be in each other's lives, why the hell weren't we?

It just seems too simple of an answer.

But it also eases the pain knowing he always wanted to be a part of my life.

I still don't understand how Penelope can live with herself, knowingly entering a man's life who has a child and purposely keeping them apart.

Planting the seed in him that he shouldn't need to be a big part of my life.

What person can sleep at night knowing they are the cause of that?

Why? Why wasn't he strong enough to stand his ground? We wouldn't have lost all of these years together.

But still, if he really wanted to be in my life, he would have just made it happen.

My brain is swirling with this new information. I don't know what to think. I don't know what to feel.

So, I do the first thing that comes to mind. I pick up my phone.

"Hi, sweetie," my mom's voice greets me, instantly soothing a part of me.

"Hi," I whisper.

"Are you crying? What's wrong?" she says with concern.

Leave it to her to know with one word that I'm not okay.

"I just got this letter from Dad's lawyer," I explain, then proceed to tell her what it said.

She takes a moment before speaking to let it all sink in. Mom never rushes to a response, choosing instead to pick her words carefully.

"How do you feel about what he wrote?" she asks gently.

I sigh into the phone, not knowing how to respond.

"I don't know," I say through tears. "I feel...angry. At him for letting it become what it did, at Penelope for getting in the way. At myself for not trying harder. I feel bad that he found himself stuck in the middle."

"That makes sense. You just read it, so it may take some time to really process it all. Don't be too hard on yourself. Just let whatever emotions come to the surface have their place. Nothing you feel is wrong."

"What did he mean when he said he wasn't in a good headspace when he left you?" I ask. "If you don't mind me asking."

"If you're asking me for my honest opinion, I think he has suffered from depression for a while. He was always looking for something to cure his woes outside of himself. It was either my fault because I wasn't adventurous enough, or the life we built was too regimented. I tried to tell him he needed help, but growing up in our generation, men were told never to open up or be vulnerable. It's a different time now."

"I see. How come you never told me that?" I ask.

"I don't know. I suppose I didn't want to put words in his mouth. It was just my opinion. After we divorced, it didn't seem like my place to tell you what I thought about him. I never wanted to make it seem like I was bad-mouthing him."

"Makes sense. I'm sure I would've just told you it's all just an excuse. To some degree, though, no matter what the reason is...it will never be good enough."

"Not at all. He should've gotten help so he could show up and be present in your life. It sounds like he knows that, and he regrets it."

"I don't know what to do," I say through another round of tears.

"You don't have to do anything right now. Just take some time to let it sink in and be gentle with yourself."

"Okay. I can do that." I take a deep breath. "I'm sorry to bother you while you're at work."

"Never apologize for calling me when you need me. I'll call you later tonight to check in. Okay?"

"Okay. I love you, Mom."

"I love you too, sweetie."

Give myself time. I can do that. I place the letter back in the envelope.

Right now, I just want to get back to work so I can get some distance from it all. That might help me sort through the spiderweb of emotions.

Chapter Twenty-Three

Asher

"Say goodnight to Charlotte," I tell Brie after she's done with her last-minute cartoon before bed.

Brie runs over to Charlotte in her onesie pajamas and gives her a hug. "Night, Charwotte."

"Goodnight, Princess."

Charlotte smiles as she hugs my daughter then Brie runs back to me.

"I'll be right back," I tell Charlotte.

As I walk Brie back to her bedroom, I start to think about all the moments we've shared with Charlotte together over the last few weeks. Brie is absolutely smitten with her, and Charlotte seems to share the same sentiment.

I don't know what it all means.

We haven't talked about our fight the other night. I keep avoiding the topic.

Truth is, I'm terrified—of many things. Terrified of getting hurt, terrified of losing her, terrified that I'm not enough for her.

But I'm also terrified that if we have a fight, it'll ruin any chance of her deciding to stay in Isle of Hope.

I had to admit that there's a part of me that wishes that when summer is over, she'll decide on her own to stay here.

And that thought, that desire, is lethal. It could take me down despite my efforts to remain neutral in this relationship we've built.

After I've read Brie her bedtime story, I kiss her forehead and wish her goodnight.

When I emerge into the living room, Charlotte isn't there. I smile. She better be in my bedroom, ready for me to take her.

But when I find her in my bedroom, my body goes rigid.

"What the hell are you doing?" my voice cuts into the silence.

She looks up with wide eyes.

"What's this?" she whispers.

"That's what you're gonna do? You're gonna ask me questions about my personal shit that you have no right going through."

I step closer, trying to control my fury.

"I didn't mean to. I was reaching for a towel in your linen closet, and this box fell down. What are all of these phone records and bank records? Were you spying on your wife? Did she do something?"

"Charlotte, that's none of your business."

She stands up and takes a step toward me.

I back away, like that's going to protect me from her onslaught of questions.

"Why won't you talk to me? Something happened between you two, something bigger than her sudden passing. Layla thinks that..."

"I don't give a damn what Layla or anybody else thinks. Why won't you just let this go?" I beg through clenched teeth.

"Because whatever happened is stopping you from healing, from moving on. From trusting others. You said it yourself the other night. You don't trust anybody. That's no way to live your life."

I can't believe she is still pushing. Can't she see what it's doing to me?

"I don't need to trust people. What I need is to protect my daughter, and that's what I'm doing," I reply sharply.

"Protect her from what? Burying secrets and hiding from your pain is not protecting anybody."

I begin to pace back and forth as my temper flares.

"Why should I tell you anyway? You're leaving in a couple weeks."

She looks shocked by my harsh assault on her. "I still care about you. I thought we were at least on the same page. I thought we meant something to each other."

"It doesn't matter." I change course, desperately trying to end this attack on my personal life. "Just forget I said anything."

"Asher, you can't hide away from this."

"I can do whatever the hell I want," I quip back.

She doesn't understand. I can't dredge this back up. I have my reasons, and no one else needs to know what they are.

"Yes, you *can* do whatever the hell you want. But I'm not going to stick around and let my heart get stomped on. I opened up to you, I cried in your arms. I let you take care of me. If you can't do the same, then..."

"Then what?" I interrupt vehemently.

If she's asking that I cry in her arms. she's crazy.

Tears begin to fall down her cheeks. "Then I can't do this anymore. I'm falling for you. I don't know if this was supposed to be a summer fling or what the intentions were, but I can't help it. And if you are just going to keep secrets and only give me a piece of your heart..." she wipes her tears away. "That's just not enough for me."

"I never promised you my secrets," I shout. "I never promised you my heart."

Her chest racks at my words then she starts for the door.

"Where the hell are you going?" I demand, hot on her tail.

"I'm not going to be treated like this. You need to figure your shit out." She grabs her purse and heads for the front door. "Call me if you decide to let me in."

Then I'm standing alone in my foyer as panic begins to build. Shit, I don't want to lose her. I can't lose her.

I can't go back to the way I felt before she came back into my life.

I pace the floor as I run my hands through my hair.

Fuck! Why does she need to know that part of my past? It's too big, too life-altering. She won't be able to keep it a secret if I tell her. She'll want to do something. She'll want to right the wrong, and I have my daughter to look after.

Was this ever going to work anyway? We have too much working against us.

My history, my pain, my trust issues. Her living situation, my inability to move because of my daughter, and the support system we've built here.

What was I thinking, letting myself get this invested in her?

But she said she's falling for me. I hate that despite how angry I was with her, I wanted to kiss the hell out of her when she spoke those words. Because, dammit, I'm falling for her. No, I've already fallen. I've already hit the ground at full speed, heart shattered into a million pieces.

Is there a part of me that longs for someone to love and to love me?

Fuck, probably. Yes.

But to move on, I would need to forgive those who wronged me. And there's no forgiving what was done. My heart is cold with anger and resentment.

Chapter Twenty-Four

Charlotte

It's been one week since the night of our fight.

The bastard won't even communicate directly with me. Josh is now handling the final stages of the home renovation.

He is outside power washing the house to get it ready for paint.

I just wanted to call Asher and scream at him for doing this to us.

Never mind me crying myself to sleep for a week, but what about Brie? Doesn't she deserve a father who is happy and emotionally stable?

I love that girl. I don't want her to grow up not trusting anyone around her because that's what she sees her father do. He will keep everyone at arm's length, and she won't know any different.

After several hours of throwing myself into my work, I decide I need to take a break.

I walk outside on the back deck to find Josh rolling up his extension cord.

"You all finished?" I ask.

"Yep. The guys should be here on Wednesday to start painting."

I look at the amount of chipped paint that the power wash got off. "Wow. I can't believe it. I can't tell whether it looks better with all of the peeling paint off or worse."

Josh chuckles. "It'll look awesome when it's done. Especially with the trim being touched up as well. Like a brand new home."

I smile as I try to picture what it will look like being restored to its original beauty. I think my dad would be happy to see it restored. I think he'd be proud.

Maybe that's why he left me the house. Maybe it meant a lot to him, too, and he wanted it to go to someone who would take care of it.

I look back at Josh, who seems to be pondering something. "So, I have to ask," he begins. "What's going on with you and Asher?"

I tilt my head to the side. "What makes you think something is going on?"

I never was good at lying. He hits me with a knowing look.

"Come on, Charlotte. He is back to being in a piss mood all the time. Worse this time. He calls me over here to handle the rest of this project when we both know something was going on between you two. He won't talk about it...and I'm done trying to get it out of him. It just makes him even more cranky."

"It just wasn't going to work between the two of us," I admit, even though the words taste sour in my mouth.

"That's a vague answer."

"He's just..." I stumble on my words, not sure what I should let out.

"Difficult," he suggests.

"Yes." I smile. "He has some things to work on before he is ready for a relationship."

"Look…we all know he hasn't dealt with some shit since Lauren passed, but don't give up on him. I know he's crazy about you. You're the motivation he needs to work through it all."

I shrug. "I don't know if my heart can handle it."

He lets out a loud sigh. "I understand. Just maybe try to be patient. I'm going to keep pushing him to get some help. He needs it."

"He didn't show any interest in getting help when I suggested it."

"He's scared. I know that deep down, he wants to be free of all of this."

"You're a good friend," I tell him, but feeling like I want out of this conversation. "Care to tell me why it is that Layla hates you so much?"

He scratches the back of his head. "Alright, you win. New subject."

I smile victoriously.

After Josh leaves, I go back to the back deck and stare up at the house. I close my eyes and try to picture what it will look like.

An image of my dad and I walking around the house and planting flowers comes to mind.

"Just like this, sweetie," he would say. "Don't be afraid to get her hands dirty."

We would dig the holes and plant the summer flowers all along the house.

"Your mom's back is hurting, but I promised her I would keep our home beautiful for her this year."

I open my eyes as I try to bite back the tears threatening to consume me. There are so many wonderful memories here with him. Memories that I've been trying to ignore since I've been here.

I think about him having depression but being too stubborn and proud to get help. The similarity to Asher is not lost on me.

If Asher has even the slightest chance with me, he needs to get help.

My dad should have gotten help for the sake of his family. But I also feel bad for him. I feel bad that he grew up in a time that wasn't kind to mental illness, particularly men with mental illness.

A memory of Dad and I chasing each other around the house with squirt guns hits me. I haven't thought about that in forever.

I laugh out loud just thinking about it. The sun shines directly down on me, engulfing my body with its warmth. It's like a giant hug.

Somehow, I just know it's my dad.

I look up at the sky and smile.

"I forgive you, Daddy," I whisper.

The weight off my chest after admitting those words out loud and really meaning them is so freeing.

I run inside, up the stairs, and into my bedroom. Pulling out the box of pictures, I move carefully around the broken glass until I find my favorite.

The picture of the three of us on the dock. My favorite spot. I take the frame down the stairs to the large family room, where there is a big gas fireplace under a huge wooden mantel.

I place the picture frame on the mantel. It's like all the pain and sorrow are replaced with happiness and gratitude. I didn't have my father for the last ten years of my life, but I'm not going to let that overshadow the seventeen years that I did have him.

Those are the years I want to remember.

I wish I knew how freeing forgiveness was. I feel like a new person. Then it dawns on me: Forgiving him was never for him; it was for me. That's the power in it—it sets the victim free, not the offender.

All these years, I hung onto my forgiveness like it was the punishment my father deserved. I couldn't let him do all those things to me and not harbor the anger he bestowed upon himself. But hanging onto the anger and resentment was only punishing me.

A couple of hours later, after I've finished work for the day, my doorbell rings.

I open it to find Layla on the other side. She storms inside, making her annoyance known by the pounding of her feet against the floors.

I close the door and follow her inside.

"So, I hear my brother's an asshole," she says as she throws her purse on the table.

I take cautionary steps further into the room, not knowing exactly what to say. This is her brother we're talking about. At the end of the day, she loves him.

"You don't have to sugarcoat anything with me," she continues. "I know he can be a pain in the ass."

"He is being stubborn," I say in agreement with her.

"I just don't understand what he's holding on to. Ugh, I wish he would open up and tell me."

I have my suspicions about what it is that happened, but I don't think it's my place to tell her.

"Josh says I should give him time. That he's going to work on getting him help."

Layla rolls her eyes. "What does Josh know? He will just turn him into a man whore like him. He needs to be healed from this pain. I hate it. I miss my brother." Her eyes begin to well up with tears. She shakes her head and fans her face. "I'm sorry. I'm a shit friend. I came here to comfort you, and here I am crying."

I lean in and give her a squeeze. "Stop it. He's your brother. You are allowed to be concerned."

"It's just..." she starts. "He was getting better when you came around. I started to see him open up again, smile, even laugh. I think I was secretly hoping that it was gonna heal him."

"I know. I saw the changes too. But one thing I can say that I've realized even with my own issues is that other people can't heal you. You have to heal yourself."

"But what if he never does that for himself?" she cries.

I sigh. "I hope he does. Not just for his sake, but for Brie's. But that's up to him."

"You're being so strong about this."

I laugh. "I've cried every night since we had our fight. But right now, I'm healing myself and my relationship with my father. I can't take on his trauma as well. This place, though, it's healing me in ways I never imagined."

I look out at the water and smile. "The view, the sun, the people."

Her head tilts to the side as she analyzes me. "Have you thought about staying for good? Maybe all this was sign that you should be here."

"I've been thinking about it. The thought of leaving here, of selling this place, it's starting to feel wrong. I don't know. It hurt to be here at first, but now it feels like it's part of me."

"You'd be okay living near my brother? Even if things don't work out?"

"It'd be hard. But this is bigger than him, bigger than us."

"Well," she smiles. "If you do stay, I promise you'll always have people here to love you. Maybe your mom could move down here eventually."

I think about that. I know mom loved this place like I do. Maybe she could eventually heal enough to move forward and see a life here.

It's a lot to consider. But life is too short to not do what makes you happy. Losing my father so suddenly, it's starting to make me see everything in a different light.

Chapter Twenty-Five

Asher

We're doing Sunday dinner at my parents' place tonight. I told Ma I needed a break. From cooking, entertaining the family... from everything.

Liam is outside with Brie, likely teaching her how to do something dangerous that I'll have to correct.

"You want a beer?" Pa asks me.

I'm sitting at their kitchen island, Layla next to me while Ma cooks.

"Yeah, thanks," I reply.

Layla hasn't talked to me yet today. She's watching me with her arms crossed, stewing on something. Probably wanting to reem me out again for not going after Charlotte.

It's been over a week.

I'm stalling. I know I am. I just don't know what to say. I'm not ready to confront everything from my past, and she won't let me off the hook. We're at an impasse, and I think I'm terrified to officially hear her tell me we're over. I'm avoiding my problems, like always.

Pa hands me the beer and I take a big gulp immediately.

Layla grunts a sound of disgust. "Just gonna sit there and drink a beer like nothing's happening."

Eric looks over at us from across the island. He was talking to Ma about something but clearly didn't miss Layla's outburst.

"Is there something we need to know?" Eric cuts in.

"Yeah. Maybe you can talk some sense into Asher. He flew off the handle at Charlotte the other night. Now he won't apologize because he's too afraid of...something."

I roll my eyes and take another sip of my beer.

"This true?" Eric asks. "You got into it with Charlotte? Were you two seeing each other?"

A muscle flicks angrily in my jaw. "It doesn't matter what we were. She's leaving at the end of the summer. It's also nobody's business what happened between us." I look at Layla when I finish.

She scoffs. "You don't even know if she wants to stay here for good or not. Probably too scared to have an honest conversation with her."

"What does that mean? If she's staying?" I ask, trying not to raise my eyebrows with such interest.

"I don't see how that's anybody's business," she says, throwing my words back at me.

I shoot her a penetrating glare.

"You know," Eric starts, "you've been different this summer. Happier. I was beginning to wonder if she had anything to do with it. I heard you were always finding a reason to be at her place."

"Your point?" I quip.

"I just think you should think really hard if whatever you two argued about is worth losing what you had this summer."

"Why is everybody assuming it was my fault?" I raise my voice.

"Well…what was the fight about?" Pa asks.

"None of anyone's damn business." I stand. "God! Why does everybody assume they know what's best for me? I'm so sick of this shit!"

I storm out of the room until I reach the front door. Once I'm outside, I begin to pace back and forth on the porch. My chest feels tight, making it hard to take in a deep breath.

It's so damn typical. They always push me like my issues are my fault, something I have control over. If they only knew.

For the first time in a long time, I'm tempted to tell them all the truth.

Maybe then they would understand why I am the way I am. Maybe they would leave me alone to make my own decisions and not judge me.

It's surprising how quickly I went back to my usual angry, grumpy self after my fight with Charlotte.

It's like she was this light in my life, in my heart, that made everything go away. Just another reason to stay away. The power she had over me was too strong, even stronger than Lauren.

I can't imagine what would happen if she ever did something to me. Would I ever recover?

Probably not, and that wouldn't be fair to Brie. Everything I do is for her. She needs to be protected from all the pain life can throw at you.

"Hi," Liam's voice echoes behind me.

I turn around as he joins me on the front porch, closing the door behind him.

"I hear I missed a little tiff in there," he says.

He takes a seat in one of the chairs, motioning for me to join him in the chair beside him.

"Talk to me," he speaks in a gentle tone.

I run a hand through my hair, then let my head fall back against the chair.

"I don't even know what to say."

"Well, I'm caught up on everything. So, why don't you start with how you're doing since you and Charlotte got into it?"

I shake my head back and forth. "Not good."

"Do you miss her?"

"Every minute," I surprise myself with my admission.

"You don't think you can work it out with her?"

I shrug as I wipe away nothing on my jeans. "She told me she can't be with me if I don't open up to her. She doesn't want any secrets."

"Are there secrets?"

"There are things that's nobody's business."

He gives me a cynical laugh. "How's that working out for ya?"

"What do you mean?" I drawl in annoyance.

He leans forward, elbows resting on his knees. "I mean, how is keeping everybody in your life at arm's length working for you?"

"It's better this way."

"So, if you see her around with another man, you'll be okay with that? You know, since it's better this way." He gives me a knowing look. "Just something to think about. Stay out here until you calm down. I'll tell everyone in there this conversation is off limits the rest of the night."

Once he's inside, I let out the ragged breath I was holding in. Fuck, just the thought of seeing her with another man.

Nothing about that feels right.

There's no way another man will please her the way I do. Will love her the way I do.

I walk back inside and hear laughter coming from the kitchen. When I walk in, Brie is dancing around to music while my family cheers her on.

"Where'd you learn to do this?" Ma asks as she watches Brie move her hands in the air.

"Charwotte." Brie spots me. "Right, Daddy?"

I can feel the sudden shift in the room. I never told anybody that Charlotte came around Brie so often. Layla may have known about the festival on the Fourth of July, but he hasn't told her about all the other nights.

"Right, sweetheart," I feign a smile as I reply.

"Alright, well, let's eat dinner," Ma breaks the silence.

The rest of the evening I stay silent. I have so many thoughts running through my brain, I can't seem to slow them down enough to even begin to understand them.

If I didn't have Brie, I would likely be drowning myself in a bottle of whiskey to drown out the noise.

It's too much.

I opt to head out as soon as dinner is over with the pretense that I need to get back home and get Brie in bed.

It's close enough to a truth that no one gives me shit. But truth be told, I need to be alone. I need some time to think about all the comments that have been thrown at me tonight.

It weighs heavy on me the entire way home. But nothing prepares me for Brie's comment at bedtime.

"Daddy?" she whispers as she hugs her teddy to her chest.

"Yeah, honey?"

"Charwotte come over tomorrow?" she asks innocently. "I miss her."

It guts me. I've never had to lie to my daughter before, and I hate that I put her in a position where I have to.

"I think Charlotte is a little busy right now with work and finishing her house."

"Oh, okay," she replies with sadness in her voice.

"Goodnight, sweetie. I'll see you in the morning."

I kiss her forehead and walk out of her room. As soon as the door is closed, I lean against the wall. My head hangs forward in defeat.

I officially don't know what the hell I'm doing anymore.

Chapter Twenty-Six

Charlotte

"This is the master bedroom," I say as I lead her in. "It has these beautiful, vaulted ceilings. And over here is the master bath."

Debra, my realtor, follows me into the bathroom as she scans it all from floor to ceiling. She nods her head for what feels like the hundredth time since she's been here.

"And that's it," I tell her. "That's the full tour."

"Very nice. It's a beautiful home. Would you like to sit down so we can go over the numbers?"

I lead her out of the bedroom, down the stairs, to my large kitchen table.

"Would you like anything to drink?" I offer as she sits. "I know this is the South, and sweet tea is a thing, but I generally try to limit my sugar. So, I can offer unsweetened tea. I don't think I have any sugar here. This has just been a temporary stay for me. If you couldn't tell by the lack of anything in the house."

She smiles warmly at me. "Unsweetened tea is perfect. Thank you."

I join her after I pour us our drinks. She pulls out some paperwork and then puts down her pen.

"So, being that the house is paid off, that does make this a lot less stressful of a process for you. We are in a sellers' market, which bodes well for you. While I do think we can come close to some of the comps in the area, we are definitely not going to be able to match or exceed them."

I take a sip as I listen.

"This is a very beautiful house, and the location right on the water will be a huge selling point. There's just not many homes with this kind of view that will pop up on the market. That being said, while the outside is freshened up, the landscaping needs work. And while the fresh paint and newly stained floors are beautiful, the bathrooms and kitchen need updating. Because of that, we will not be able to be super competitive with other houses on the market."

It's something I knew would be an issue but when she tells me how far down that could drive my price, I'm a little surprised.

"It's the kitchen," she tells me. "Bathrooms that need some updating can be a bit of a burden, but nothing like remodeling a kitchen."

"I see. I know the kitchen needs some work. I just didn't really know it was going to be that big of a price reducer."

"Well, you could always remodel it first, then sell it. That way, you know you're getting top dollar for the sale. Just something to think about."

She begins to go into more detail about what the numbers could be if I were to first remodel the kitchen and bathrooms, but I start to get lost in thought. The more she talks about selling it, the more my uneasiness grows.

I don't know what it is. Maybe it's that I've faced my past and healed a part of me that was wounded, but the thought of selling doesn't feel like it used to.

Do I want to stay here? Live in Isle of Hope?

It's not at all what I had planned, but I can't deny that being here has felt different. I feel lighter and happier. Well, I did until Asher put a little wrench in my happiness. But still, even with the heartache, it feels easier to deal with here. I have my favorite spots to center myself when everything feels like it's too much.

I always felt that when I came here for the summer. It was one of the reasons losing this place was so hard.

"So," Debra interrupts my thoughts, "what are you thinking? Would you like me to schedule my photographer to come out here and take the photos?"

I should say yes. That's what I planned all along. That's what this summer was about.

"Umm, can I get back to you on that? I want to give some thought to updating the kitchen before I commit."

"Absolutely. You take all the time you need."

After she packs up her things and leaves me with her information, I begin to pace around the house. My stomach begins to ache with my indecision. I hate not knowing what to do. How do I even make this decision?

I need to talk to someone. I pick up my phone and immediately dial my mom.

"Hi, sweetie," her cheerful voice greets me.

"I need help," I blurt out.

"Talk to me," she replies.

I sigh. "The realtor just left."

"Ah," she says with what sounds like understanding. "How did it go?"

"I mean, the house is definitely in good enough shape to sell. She did tell me I could get a lot more money for it if I upgrade the kitchen and bathrooms."

"Well, that's good. I'm proud of you for getting it in good enough shape for resale this summer. Do you want to stay and finish the rest before you sell?"

"I don't know, Mom. When I thought about getting rid of this place in the beginning, it felt good. To be honest, I couldn't get rid of it fast enough. Now, when I think about selling," I trail off, struggling to find the words. "I just don't know if I want to sell it anymore."

"What do you think changed?"

I look around, taking in the feel of warmth in my body that it creates.

"It just feels like home. You know? It always did for me. That's why it was so hard for me to lose this place. That's why I was filled with so much anger when it was ripped away from me. Now that I'm here, now that I've healed from it all, it just reminds me of how happy I've always been when I was here."

"You did always shine your brightest those summers we were there," she says with reverence.

"You noticed that?"

"I did. Your laugh was always a little louder, your smile a little bigger. Your energy was different there."

"So, you think I should stay?"

"I can absolutely understand if that's what you decide. I'll support any of your decisions. But you need to make this decision on your own."

I let out an audible breath. "I know I do." I glance out the window from the kitchen to the dock. My favorite spot in the entire world. If there's any place I can make this decision, it's there. "It helps just knowing that you'd support my decision. Thanks, Mom."

"Of course. Let me know when you decide. You'll know the right decision. I'm sure you already do."

We chat for a bit more about how things are going with family back home and what she's been up to this summer. When I hang up with her, I make myself a cup of coffee. Am I ready to leave behind an entire life I'd built back in Cincinnati? It's not at all what I had planned when I decided to spend my summer here.

I walk outside and down the rocky steps built into the grass until I reach the dock. As I walk down to the end, my body settles. All my nerves and uncertainty begin to fade away.

The warmth of the coffee soothes me as I sit down and take in the view.

I try to let myself think back to all the feelings I initially had on the way here. The anger in my body was so fierce, so consuming. The way the neglect of the house signified the neglect I felt all those years from my father.

Maybe repairing the house was also my way of repairing our relationship.

With each paint chip removed, I made room for a new coat—a new feeling to come through.

But was this summer about healing and not staying?

That's the question.

I try to imagine what it would feel like to officially hand over the keys to this place, to know I would never be able to come back.

One thing is for sure: whatever my decision is, this summer was meant to be.

Chapter Twenty-Seven

Asher

There hasn't been an overcast day in weeks. And yet, here I stand outside of my car, looking at the grey skies. It matches my mood as I look out at the vast green land in front of me.

I haven't been here since the day my wife was buried.

Does that make me a bad man?

But how could I when the truth of her unfaithfulness was revealed to me only *after* her death?

I can still remember how it felt to be missing her so much that I could hardly breathe. I was in our bed as our eleven-month-old daughter was napping in her crib, asking God why he would take a mother away from her baby.

I opened her nightstand drawer to pull out her perfume. I wanted to spray it on her pillow so I could feel like she was still next to me.

Instead, I found her cell phone. I thought reading her messages would make me feel close to her.

I was wrong. Opening up her phone, reading her messages, it changed me forever.

The man who once trusted and loved openly became bitter and resentful. I became someone who never knew who was capable of hurting me.

In the end, I figured it was everyone. Everyone held the power to hurt me.

So, I closed my heart off from every person in my life. The only one who it opened up for was Brielle. And for the longest time, I was okay with that.

I felt safe with that plan.

Now, with Charlotte in my life, it feels like I can no longer ignore the pain that was caused by her indiscretions. I deserve my chance to say what I want to say.

I walk down the long line of gravestones. The numbers continue to get higher, pointing me in the direction of the stone toward the end.

I stop in front of it. Hands in my pockets, my head hangs low as I read the stone.

Lauren Williams

Devoted wife and mother.

I shake my head, remembering how angry I was when I had to pick out the gravestone. It was months after she had passed, and I had just found out about her affair.

After delaying for too long, her mother eventually told me what to write. She thought I was just too deep in my grief to get anything done.

But I couldn't find it in my heart to tell her the truth. Mainly for Brielle's sake. I never wanted her to grow up in a world where her mother's name would be tarnished.

She will already have to deal with growing up without her mother. Adding that to her life just seemed unnecessary.

No, it was my cross to bear. And bear I have for the last two years.

I glance back down at the words that will forever sting.

Devoted wife. I couldn't get over how that was going to be on her stone forever when it wasn't true.

"How could you do it?" I ask as I feel my body flood with anger but, most of all—sadness.

"It wasn't even one time. Not a drunken mistake. Not a momentary lapse in judgment. Those text messages went back six months before you were sick, and they didn't stop until the day you found out you were sick."

I close my eyes as images of her with another man flood my brain.

"Just because you ended it when you found out you were sick doesn't absolve you from your mistakes. You spent three months knowing you were going to die, knowing you could've told me the truth, and you didn't."

My body begins to shake as I realize tears are now spilling down my cheeks. It dawns on me that I've never cried over her betrayal. The anger gripped me like a chokehold, not allowing me to move on.

I squat down to get closer to the ground, letting my hand trace over the word wife. My tears threaten to choke me as I gasp for more air.

"What did I do wrong?" I cry. "Why the hell would you do that to me? To our family? We just had a baby together. Who the hell does that?"

I think back to the times she ran out to "get more diapers" or "needed a girl's night out."

Was she with him?

While I was rocking our baby girl to sleep, she was out with another man. Part of me has always wondered if she was dealing with some postpartum issues that she didn't know how to deal with. She seemed different after our baby arrived. I just figured those nights out with the girls were gonna help her get back to who she was before.

It just never made sense, her affair. It still doesn't make sense. We were happy. I know we were. From the moment we found out she was pregnant; we were on cloud nine.

At least I was. Maybe I missed all the warning signs, telling me she wasn't happy.

"I'm not going to let your decisions ruin my life anymore," I tell her. "It's been long enough. I'm moving on, Lauren."

I pull our wedding rings out of my pocket and place them in the vase attached to her gravestone.

"I'll always speak highly of you to our daughter. She will always know who her mother was, but my heart is no longer yours."

When I'm back in my car, I lie my head back and close my eyes. Charlotte's face is the first thing I see.

Her face is the first thing that I see in the morning and the last thing I see before I fall asleep. She consumes my thoughts all day, every day.

She's the reason I'm here, the reason I'm forcing myself to confront my demons head-on.

As I drive my car along the dark, gloomy streets, I begin to feel lighter. It's freeing to have finally spoken to her about what she did. Even if she couldn't talk back, I still felt heard.

Finding out that the person you committed your life to deceived you in the worst possible way only after they're gone is a torture I wouldn't wish on anyone.

It's impossible to sort out your feelings. Every negative thought or feeling you have toward them feels wrong since they're gone. It just leads to so much anger and resentment at the world in general since you can't focus it on the offender. I know this doesn't solve everything, but it's a start. For the first time, it gives me hope that I can find a way out of this trap I've created around my heart.

Chapter Twenty-Eight

Charlotte

"Did you seriously say that to him?" I gasp at Layla.

We're walking through the department store with a fresh cup of coffee in our hands. I spent all week trying to figure out what I wanted when it all finally hit me while sitting on the dock one morning.

"He was being a total jackass," she defends. "He's lucky I didn't kick him out of my restaurant."

"Have you ever done that before? Kicked him out?" I ask.

She and Josh have had such an on-and-off relationship since I've come around. I honestly can't tell anymore whether they really hate each other or not.

"No," she sighs. "But I should. Anyway," she takes a sip of her coffee, "care to tell me why I met you here to walk around with a cup of coffee on a Saturday morning? I mean, I'm not complaining or anything, but I don't think I've ever been asked to have coffee while doing this."

I laugh, thinking about how strange of a request it is without any context. "I appreciate you going along with it. Though, there is a reason for it."

She looks at me skeptically. "Spit it out already."

"I've decided to stay in Isle of Hope. Permanently."

"What?" she squeals. "Are you serious?"

I nod my head. Layla wraps her arms around me. "You have no idea how happy this makes me. When did you decide?"

"Yesterday morning," I tell her as we stand in the middle of the aisle. "I met with a realtor recently, and the entire time, I had this horrible feeling in the pit of my stomach. The truth is, I don't want to move. This place has always been a safe haven for me. I love it. And I don't want to give up the last place that I feel connected to my dad."

She smiles sadly. "I get it. It's a special place for you."

"And...now that I'm staying. I need some furniture."

She looks around in understanding. "Ahhh. So today is a day of shopping? Well, you've asked the right person to help. Now tell me, what exactly are we looking for?"

I try to think of all the things floating around in my brain. There's so much to buy, and I know I can't afford all of it at once.

"I want to get a coffee table and end tables for the family room. I need some furniture for the master bedroom. I plan on bringing my current bed and furniture down here to use in a spare bedroom for when my mom visits. I need some new appliances for the kitchen. I think that's where I'm starting today."

"You picked a good spot. Between here and the rest of the stores on this strip, we can do some serious damage."

"That's what I'm hoping," I tell her. "I'm super excited to make the place my own."

As we walk around the store, picking things out, Layla awkwardly turns to me. I can tell she isn't sure how to say whatever she's going to say. And I'm pretty sure I know who it's about.

"So, have you told my brother that you're staying?" she finally asks.

"No," I let out a breath of frustration. "I can't deal with him right now. I need to make these decisions for myself. I've spent enough nights crying myself to sleep over him. If he wants to talk to me, he can call me."

"Ugh, he pisses me off." Her annoyance is evident. "I told him off the other day. He needs to get his head out of his ass and get some help."

I stop in my tracks in between furniture to look at her. "You said that to him?"

"Yes. I'm just so frustrated. I can't sit back and watch him crumble without speaking up. He's done it long enough, and he needs to hear it."

I know I should be glad that people are trying to make him get help, but I'm also a little worried. I love him, and I don't want him to be pushed too far if he's not ready.

"I hope he's okay. Do you think someone should be checking on him?" I ask.

"He sees my parents every day. He's tough, I know he can survive it all, but I just want him to do more than survive life. You know?"

"I get it."

I do get it. No one wants to see him live life in pain. Brie deserves more than that. He deserves more than that.

I hate thinking about them. It just brings back the empty part of me that I've felt since the fight. I didn't expect to fall in love with Brie so quickly, but it happened.

There was this instant connection I felt with her. Like her and I were meant to be in each other's lives.

But I can't force him to come to me and be ready to open up, and I'm standing my ground. I can't be with someone who won't open their heart to me.

"Let's not talk about my brother anymore. Today is about celebrating. We are going to find you the perfect furniture and make your house everything you want it to be. Then, we're going to go out and celebrate tonight. How does that sound?"

I smile at her. "I love the sound of that. Where do you think we should go tonight?"

"I'll have to think about that. Oh, look at this bedroom set," she says, completely distracted.

A night out is exactly what I need. I've been wallowing at night without Asher, and it's time I put a stop to that. It's not healthy for me to stare at my phone, willing it to ring. It's been weeks, and he hasn't called. I need to move on with my life because I can't sit around waiting for him if he isn't ready. Who knows if he will ever be.

Chapter Twenty-Nine

Asher

I just put Brie in bed about thirty minutes ago. It's been a hell of a day. She refused her nap this afternoon and has been hell on wheels ever since.

Everything I said or did seemed to piss her off. It was like walking on eggshells around her, not knowing what was going to create another tantrum.

Luckily, she was out before I even left the room. She rarely falls asleep during story time, but she couldn't keep her eyes open.

I finally find a good movie to watch when my phone buzzes next to me.

Josh: Out for the night. Layla wanted to celebrate the good news about Charlotte. We're at Social Club if you want to join.

I want to ask what news he's talking about, but I hesitate. Why are they celebrating? Did she sell the house already?

A knot forms in the pit of my stomach. I knew it was coming. I just didn't know it would happen so fast.

What if I went after her? I could've changed her mind and made her stay.

But I can't do that. I can't go after her and ask that of her when I'm in this kind of shape. If she wants a man who can open his heart, that's not me.

At least not yet. The first step at Lauren's grave was monumental for me, but just the tip of the iceberg.

> Me: I don't think she wants me there. I wouldn't blame her. I wouldn't want me there either.

He texts back instantly.

> Josh: Paul sure seems to be happy that you're not here.

That motherfucker.

Josh knows exactly what he's doing. He's goading me, and it's fucking working. I know I don't have any right to claim her as mine right now, but dammit, she is mine.

I love her.

And he just wants what's mine.

On the way to my room, I whip off my shirt and find a new faded red one to put on. It's my favorite baseball shirt that I've had forever. I throw on a hat and text my brothers.

> Me: I need someone to come here and hang at my place while Brie sleeps. It's urgent.

I begin pacing back and forth as I picture his hands on her.

> Eric: I can be there in ten. Is everything alright?

> Me: Just get here soon. No one's hurt if that's what you're worried about.

Just as promised, he's pulling in my driveway within ten minutes. I open the front door as he approaches.

"This isn't like you," he says as he comes in. "Care to tell me what's so urgent?"

I lift my hat and run my hand through my hair. "It's just...hard to explain. Charlotte."

He nods his head in understanding. "That sounds kinda easy to explain to me. Get outta here. I've got it covered."

"Thanks," I say with relief. "I won't be too late."

He shrugs as if when I'm home is no concern to him.

The entire drive to the bar, I try to rack my brain with a reason to be there, but I've got nothing.

The damn truth is, I shouldn't be going. I'm too messed up in the head to be her man right now, and she doesn't owe me a thing.

I'm also too in love with her to let her go. What am I going to do? Beg her to stay and wait around for me to work on myself. No woman in the world would want to do that.

I park my car and practically run into the bar. I spot them outside in the back corner.

Layla and Josh are bickering about something, acting like it's not some years-long foreplay that none of us can see through.

Avery and Kyle are all over each other. Someone needs to talk to them about their excessive PDA.

Josh and Layla spot me, and I see the shock on Layla's face as I approach.

"What're you doing here?" she asks.

I shrug. "Just thought I'd come by. I hear there's a celebration tonight."

Layla crosses her arms. "There is. But I'm not sure you should be here. Charlotte just told me today and I wanted tonight to be about her."

I squeeze my fists to try to reign in my frustration.

"I'm surprised you're celebrating her selling the house and leaving," I reply.

Layla turns her head to the side. "That's not what we're celebrating."

I stiffen up. "What are you celebrating?"

She gives me her *I'm annoyed with you* face again. "Not that it's any of your business, but Charlotte decided not to sell. She's going to live here permanently."

I'm completely caught off guard. I don't know what to do with the information or how to process it. I can pinpoint one emotion for sure: relief.

Charlotte isn't leaving.

It's like a breath of fresh air.

As if my body can sense her, I look passed Layla and see Charlotte and Avery talking. Charlotte's eyes keep wandering over to me.

I can't quite gauge what she's thinking or feeling about my presence. The woman who is normally an open book to me has her guard up, and I hate it.

"I had no idea," I tell Layla, not knowing what else to say.

"Just don't make tonight about you guys. Maybe offer her a congratulations and keep it at that. Okay?" she begs.

I nod in understanding. "I don't want to ruin her night any more than you do. I'm gonna go get a beer."

The entire time I'm waiting in line for my drink, I try to work out the news of Charlotte's living situation in my head. I wonder if there's a chance part of her decision was about me. Maybe I haven't fucked things up so badly that we're a total lost cause. A glimmer of hope forms in my chest.

When I walk back outside with my beer, the three girls are laughing together. It doesn't feel like a good time to approach Charlotte, so I find Josh.

"Glad you could make it," he says to me as he slaps me on the shoulder.

"I'm not an idiot. I know what you were trying to do with that text," I fire back at him.

He takes a big sip of his drink, seemingly unbothered. "It got you here, didn't it?"

"That it did. I'm surprised you want me here to witness your little love fest with my sister," I quip.

His arm stops with his beer midway to his mouth, completely shocked that I said what I said. I don't know, maybe it's that I'm desperate to get the focus off me, but I've never broached the subject with him.

He seems pissed. "There's nothing going on between me and your sister, dick. She hates me."

I cock an eyebrow at him. "What's the saying? There's a thin line between love and hate."

"Don't deflect your shit onto me. Trust me, Layla hates my guts."

I look back at Charlotte, who is watching me intently.

But then, out of nowhere, Paul appears.

He has no idea I'm here. I watch as he takes a seat next to Charlotte, wraps his arm around her neck, and whispers in her ear. The entire time, her eyes remain on me.

I've held in my anger for years, kept it hidden. Right now, I don't know what the difference is. Maybe it's that I'm starting to release some of the anger that's making it unable to stop the rest of it from pouring out.

I storm over to the two of them and shove him off the table onto the ground.

"Dude, what the fuck was that for?" he looks up at me.

"That's for putting your hands on my girl," I growl. "You'd be wise to keep your hands to yourself from now on."

His eyes darken. "Last I heard, she wasn't your girl."

Once he's back on his feet, he gets closer to me with a challenging look.

"She's mine," I reiterate, making sure he understands.

Charlotte looks between us. "It's fine, Asher. We were just talking."

"Yeah, we were just talking," Paul advances. "Butt out. It's none of your business."

My entire body fills with the all-too-familiar rage. "It's my business. It was my business when you fucked my wife, and it's my business now."

The gasps around me let me know that we have an audience, but I don't give a shit anymore. I tried to keep it a secret, tried to protect Lauren's honor, but I'm done.

Paul's face tells me he's shocked. He had no clue I was aware that it was him.

"She told you?" he questions.

"It doesn't fucking matter how I know. All that matters is that you're a slimy piece of shit who ruins people's lives. I don't know how you sleep at night, knowing you slid in and fucked my wife repeatedly while I was taking care of our baby girl at home."

"Is that fucking true, man?" Josh interrupts with a look of fury on his face.

Paul looks at him, looks at everyone watching, then shrugs. "She wanted it."

Before I can even move in on him, Charlotte is in his face. I see her arm wind up then her fist close in on Paul's nose.

He falls back, covering his face as he screams. "What the hell, Charlotte?"

"You prick," she yells at him.

He pulls his hands away, and there's blood running down his face. Shit. My girl can pack a punch. I shouldn't be enjoying this as much as I am, but that was probably the hottest thing I've ever seen in my life.

"You're lucky I don't come after you for more," she threatens as she advances on him.

"Okay," Layla pulls her back. "As much as I'd love to see you do that again, let's not get thrown in jail for assault."

"All these years," Josh looks between me and Paul. "You've kept this a secret?"

I realize he's speaking to me. "I didn't know how to tell anyone. There's a lot of reasons."

"And you," Josh turns his venom to Paul. "You've had the nerve of coming around after what you did."

"Lauren was mine first." Paul wipes the blood off him with his shirt. "I was the one who met her in the bar."

"I don't give a shit who she talked to first. This wasn't some kindergarten *finders-keeper's* shit. They were married. They had a child," Josh screams.

Part of me was afraid if I brought it to light, no one would be as enraged as I was. But watching Josh now, and seeing Charlotte throw that punch, it makes me realize how foolish I was for second-guessing the people in my life.

"Hey," I step in, realizing there's no point. He is clearly not sorry for his actions. "It's not worth it. Let's just walk away."

Josh turns me, first with a look of frustration, then understanding. He nods his head at me before he turns back to Paul. "Don't even think of showing your face around us again."

Paul mumbles some cuss words as he walks away, the crowd around us watching him go.

I think I'm in shock. I don't know how long I stand in place just trying to process what just happened. I turn behind me and see Charlotte sitting on the picnic table bench holding her hand.

I'm in front of her in seconds. "Are you okay?" I ask as I squat down, gently taking her hand in mine.

"Yeah," she flinches. "My hand is killing me."

I take a look at it and see the swelling already starting on her knuckles. Damn, this girl can throw a punch.

"It doesn't look broken," I say as I inspect. "Josh, can you go get some ice from the bartender?"

"Absolutely," he says as he turns and runs inside.

"I can't believe you did that," I tell her as I look up at her beautiful face.

She smiles down at me. "That asshole deserved it."

I smile back. "I can't argue with that."

"Here you go," Josh says as he hands me a bag of ice.

"Thanks." I take the bag from him. "This is gonna hurt," I tell Charlotte as I hold the bag just above her knuckles.

She nods her head for me to continue. I lay it on as gentle as I possibly can, but that doesn't stop her whimpering from the pain.

"Can I drive you home?" I ask her, feeling desperate to be alone with her.

"Yes," she whispers.

I lift her up and start to walk away.

"Hey," Layla calls from behind. "I'm sorry. I had no idea."

I shake my head. "I know. We'll talk tomorrow," I reassure her.

Chapter Thirty

Charlotte

He lifts me into his truck, and I enjoy the feeling of his hands on me again. I know it doesn't mean anything, he's just taking me home, but there's a part of me that desperately wants this to be more.

When he closes the door, I sit in the dark on my own while he walks around the car. The ice pack rests on my hand, giving some minor relief to the pain. I've never punched someone before, but it's good to know if I'm angry enough, I could take a man down. Well, I wouldn't say I took him down. He stumbled, but I made him bleed. That has to count for something.

I honestly don't know what happened. I was filled with such outrage over what he did that my body seemed to act before my brain could catch up. I feel like I blacked out there for a moment.

But in truth, I'm glad I hit that motherfucker.

Sleeping with his friend's wife while they just had a baby together. What a dick!

I watch as Asher slides into the driver's seat and starts up the car. We sit in silence for a minute, neither of us speaking the first word.

He eventually takes a deep breath and looks over at me. I look into his green eyes which hold so much pain and yet so much adoration right now.

It makes my heart beat erratically.

"How's your hand doing?" he asks.

I can't believe he is worried about my hand. It should be him we are talking about. It shows that beyond the pain and anger that he has held onto, there is truly an amazing man beneath.

"My hand doesn't matter. How are you doing right now?"

He just shrugs his shoulders like what happened doesn't matter. He's doing it again. He's trying to close back up and keep it all inside. I don't know why I thought it would be any different. He's still the same guy he was a week ago.

I huff out a breath of frustration. "Can you just take me home, please?"

But he doesn't move. I feel him study me for a moment while I refuse to meet his eyes. It's too painful.

"I don't know how I'm doing," he begins hesitantly. "I'm pissed as hell that it finally came out, and he didn't show a lick of remorse. The bastard ruined my life but had the balls to tell me she *wanted it*. I hate that I didn't get to punch him, and *you* are the one hurting from it. I'm angry that my so-called wife did this to me. But in some sense," he pauses, then sighs. "I don't know, maybe a little relieved that the truth is out. Does that sound crazy?"

This poor man. Feeling guilty for feeling relieved. "Of course, you're relieved, Asher. No one should have to hold onto such a painful secret. And to think that you've been around him for *years* without saying a thing. I don't know how you did it." I meet his eyes. "Why did you do it?"

"Brie," he says on a breath. "She already has to navigate life without a mother. I just didn't want her to also have a bad impression of who her mother was. And I guess, also... I was embarrassed. I mean, my own wife was fucking my friend behind my back when we had a newborn baby. What does that say about me as a husband?"

I'm irritated for him right now. Why the hell would she do that? Asher was clearly a devoted husband and father. Not only to cheat on your husband but with one of his friends.

"The only thing that says about you is that you were a committed husband and father. You did nothing wrong in this scenario. Everything you're feeling is normal. And I get why you didn't want Brie to find out, but that's just not fair to you to bottle it up. Plus, it's not like she needs to know. I mean, it's not like any of your family and friends are going to tell her, so it can still be kept a secret from her if you want."

He smiles. "Thanks, Charlotte. Even after how I've treated you, you're still willing to be so kind. You're an incredible woman."

"I get it. I was snooping in your personal business when I shouldn't have. But I just wanted you to open up to me the way I opened up to you."

He nods his head. "I know. And just so you know, I'm working on it. I know I'm not the man you deserve right now, but I wanna be. I'm trying to move on from all of this crap. Maybe one day, if I'm lucky, I'll be that man for you."

Tears run down my cheeks at his words. It's what I desperately want, but I know I can't wait around for it. That would tear me apart. I have to live my life like it's not going to happen in order for me to put one foot in front of the other.

"Can you take me home?" I request again through my thick emotions.

I see the disappointment my answer causes him, but I don't want to give him any false hope. This time, he listens to my request and puts the truck in reverse.

The entire ride to my house is spent in silence. I want to say more, but I'm afraid. I'm weak around this man, and too much time alone could lead to something that shouldn't happen.

When he pulls into my driveway, I start to get out of his truck, thinking he's just dropping me off. But he kills the engine and follows me to the door.

"You don't have to walk me to the door," I tell him.

He looks at me like I'm crazy. "I'm not. I'm coming inside."

"Excuse me?" I ask, not sure how to take his forwardness.

"You just punched the man who slept with my wife. Your hand is swollen, bruised, and I can tell you're in pain. I'm coming in to get you settled in for the night. It's the least I can do."

I smile. "I thought you were mad that I was the one who got to punch him and not you."

He chuckles. "I'm willing to forgive you. Seriously, just let me come in and help. I'll feel better if I can do that."

As soon as we're inside, he tells me to go sit on the couch while he gets more ice.

"Where are your painkillers?" he asks from the kitchen.

"In the cabinet to the left of the fridge."

He's walking back toward me with a glass of water, pills, and a fresh bag of ice tucked under his arm.

I take the pills down easily, then place the glass on my new end table, coaster underneath, of course. These cost a pretty penny, so I'm gonna be anal as fuck about it, and I don't even care.

When it's time for the new bag of ice, I cringe.

"I know, it's gonna suck for a minute. But when it eventually numbs it, doesn't it feel better?"

"Yes, but that doesn't negate the initial pain."

"Come on," he sits next to me. "Give me your hand."

I do so, and he places it gently on his leg while he shakes his head.

"I still can't believe you got in such a good punch. Have you ever hit somebody before?"

I shake my head. "Never."

"Well, remind me never to piss you off."

I chuckle. "You've already done it plenty of times."

"True. I guess I'm just lucky you've spared me."

He places the ice, and I grit my teeth, waiting for the initial pain to subside. I can't think straight when the pain is throbbing so intensely on my hand.

"I went to Lauren's grave for the first time," he blurts out.

I think it's in an effort to distract me, and it works.

"What?" I choke out through the pain.

"I told you I'm trying to navigate this mess of a life I'm living. I thought the first step was to finally make it to her grave. She was my wife, the mother of my child, and I hadn't been there since the day we lowered her into the ground." He laughs bitterly. "I'm sure that makes me an asshole."

I feel for him. What a tough situation to be put in. He looks at me with pleading eyes.

"Not an asshole. You were hurt by someone you trusted. You needed time."

He sighs. "I yelled at her. I showed up at her grave for the first time in years and yelled at her."

"You needed to get it out. You've been put in an impossible situation. Nothing you say or do makes you a bad person. You need to give yourself a break while you navigate this."

"Thanks, Charlotte," he says weakly. "I don't deserve your kindness right now. I'm so sorry for how I reacted the last time we were together. You found the research I had done when I found the text messages between Lauren and Paul. I had become obsessed for a while, going through bank statements and anything I could get my hands on. I just wanted it to be stuffed in a box and to go away without dealing with it, and I took it out on you."

"I forgive you. There's no need to rehash it right now."

My hand is finally starting to go numb again, giving me the much-needed relief from the pain. Although, the pain of the man I love sitting in front of me and not being able to touch him, to kiss him, is a pain that's a thousand times more difficult to bear.

I look away from him as I will myself not to cry.

"I'm serious what I said," he tells me. "I want to become the man that can deserve your love. Because I do love you."

A sob escapes me instantly hearing him say those words. I can't look at him.

"Please, don't say that. I can't—I can't hear it right now. Please," I beg. "I just need space. I do hope you can find peace with everything—you deserve it. But if I wait around for it to happen, and something gets in the way, I just won't survive it. So, for right now, it just needs to be goodbye."

I still can't look at him, but the shift of energy in the room is evident. I feel his eyes on me as I look down at my hands, tears running down my cheeks.

"I'm so sorry, Charlotte. I'll," he cuts off as I hear his own tears break free, "I'll let myself out."

He gets up off the couch. The further he goes, the more desperate I feel to beg him to stay. It's a battle between my brain and my heart. My body wants to listen to my heart, which is telling me to go after him, to ask him to stay with me.

I can't get those words out because, although I love him, I love myself, too. And I know what is best for me right now.

Instead, I lie down on the couch and let the tears take over. Sobs wreck me as I cry over the man that I've wanted since I was seventeen.

I don't know how long I lay here and let the tears fall, but eventually, the exhaustion of my emotions takes over, and I drift into sleep.

Chapter Thirty-One

Asher

"Get over here," Ma says the second Brielle and I walk through the door on Sunday.

She takes Brie from me and engulfs me in the biggest hug she's ever given me. Her sniffling in my ear lets me know she's crying.

"Why didn't you tell me?" she cries.

"I don't know, Ma," I cry with her. "Several reasons, I guess."

She pulls away, wiping her face while Brie looks at us with concern.

"Daddy and Grawma sad," she states as she continues to look between us.

I try to blink away my own tears, embarrassed that I've cried so many times in the last forty-eight hours.

"It's okay. We are fine, sweetie," I reassure her.

We walk into the kitchen where the rest of my family is. It's quiet as everyone watches me with pitiful looks.

Liam doesn't hesitate. He just barrels into my arms.

"Fuck, dude. I wish you would've told me. I would've kicked that fucker's ass a long time ago."

I chuckle in his arms. "Thanks, not saying I wouldn't have loved to see that."

We pull away, and I turn to see everyone else still watching.

"Sorry, guys. I know I shouldn't have kept it a secret. I know it must suck to have found out how everyone did."

Layla is next to hop in my arms. "All this time, we've been hanging out with him like it was nothing. I'm so sorry."

"It's fine. You didn't know," I say, realizing I'm easing everyone else's worries.

It's incredible how much a secret can affect so many people. It was eating me alive on the inside and changing me, making my family sick with worry.

"How are you feeling?" my dad asks.

I move further into the kitchen and rest against the countertop.

"After everything, you'd think I'd feel worse than I do. I'm actually feeling a bit lighter, to be honest."

"I'm relieved to hear that," Eric says. "You seemed a little rough when you came home the other night."

My chest tightens when I think about it. "Yeah, that was more about Charlotte."

"What?" Layla freaks out. "What about her?"

"Nothing you have to worry about. It was just hard to walk away from her, but I know I'm not ready to give myself to someone yet. Actually, I've booked an appointment with a therapist. I want to get there for her, but she couldn't promise to wait for me."

"If it's meant to be, she'll wait," Ma replies. "But right now, you just need to focus on being healthy for yourself."

"Yeah, and she's here for good. She isn't going anywhere. I know Charlotte, and she's totally crazy for you."

"We'll see," I reply, not able to think about the possibility of officially losing her.

I need to be able to function and breathe for Brie, and the thought of losing Charlotte would do just that. I wouldn't be able to function. I've barely been getting by without her, but the motivation to win her back is keeping me going.

"Josh told me you were a ball of nerves that night after we left," I say to Layla.

She tenses at my words and refuses to meet my eyes.

Weird.

"Uh, yeah. I was really pissed. It all happened so fast, then you were just gone," she says to the ground.

"Well, I'm glad he was there with you."

"Mmhmm," she grumbles.

I get this odd feeling that something happened between Josh and Layla that night. She's acting weird about it. Did they get in an even bigger blowout than just their normal bickering?

I'm gonna have to address their stupidity at another time when I've dealt with my own.

Wouldn't it be nice if we all lived in a world where we weren't scared shitless to feel our feelings?

2 months later

"It's nice to see you again, Asher," Irene says from her seat.

"Nice to see you, too," I reply as I take my own.

"How was your week?" she asks.

"Well," I take a breath. "I took the boat out again."

"Good for you. That's been several weeks in a row. I'm glad you're getting out there and enjoying yourself."

"Yeah. I took my whole family on the boat this time."

"That's a big step. What? You seem uncomfortable about something?"

"I haven't been honest about something this entire time," I finally admit.

She sits up straighter. "I'm listening."

"Each time I go, I take the boat passed Charlotte's house. Sometimes she's on the dock and just the sight of her calms me. When I dropped my family off after the boat ride, I asked my sister to take Brie back to my place while I ran a few errands." My hands grip each other as I continue. "But I lied. I wanted to take the boat by her place to see if she was there."

Irene gives me a small smile. "That seems to be something that was weighing on you."

"Yeah, I don't know. I guess I felt guilty for leaving it out. Also, maybe guilty for doing it. It feels like stalking."

"I don't think I would qualify that as stalking."

"It sure feels like it."

"Why do you think you do it?"

"Because I miss her. I love her, and I just like to see her happy. She just sits there with her drink and smiles out at the water. It makes me smile. I remember she used to sit on the edge of that dock with her dad all the time, and I'd see her when I was on my father's boat. I just know how much that place means to her, and I like sharing it with her. Even if just from a distance, it makes me feel close to her."

"You've made a lot of progress since we first started. Do you feel like you're ready to talk to her about everything?"

"Do you think I'm ready?" I ask hopefully.

She chuckles. "I asked you first. I want you to tell me what you think."

Sometimes this therapy shit is annoying. They always want to know what I think or what I feel when I'd really like her to tell me what the answer is.

"I..." I stop as I try to formulate an answer. "I want to be ready. I think I've come a long way, and I know I'm in a better spot. It doesn't scare me anymore to open up to her. But I'm anxious. Sometimes I worry that I'm too anxious to open up."

She nods her head as I speak. "You have come a long way. I can sense that you worry that approaching too soon could ruin things, but I think you're ready. If the idea of opening up to her doesn't scare you, that is exactly what you said you wanted to get out of these sessions."

"It is?" I ask, not quite remembering our first session. I saw her three times a week for the first couple of weeks, but that was two months ago.

"Yes. I wrote it down. I asked you what you wanted to get out of my sessions, and you said you wanted the idea of sharing your deepest feelings with the woman you love, not to terrify you."

"Wow."

I don't know what else to say.

"I'm proud of you. You've put in the work in these sessions. You were willing to go deep and be vulnerable. It starts with me, now you need to apply that with the people you care most about."

After we finish our session, I walk out with a renewed energy. I've run into Charlotte a time or two over the last couple of months, but it was always brief. Just a friendly, 'How are you doing?'

Each time left me aching with the need to touch her, to kiss her.

Now, I actually get to offer her everything she deserves. A man who can give his heart to her. A feeling of dread takes over when I think about the possibility of her saying no.

I know she's single. I only ask Layla every time I see her. But what if the time away made her change her mind entirely?

I decide to drive straight to Josh's job site that he's working on. I've been doing these sessions during work hours so I don't have to spend more time away from Brie. She already took it hard when Charlotte stopped coming around. I didn't want her to get more confused.

It's already hard for her to grow up without a mother.

Just as I'm pulling into the office building that we're renovating completely, I see Josh walking to his truck.

He spots me from a distance and waves me over.

"What's happening?" he pats me on the back. "I was just gonna take a little break."

"Not much. I uh," I say as I rub the back of my neck, "was hoping you can help me brainstorm some things."

"I'm your guy. What are we trying to figure out?"

I lean against the back of his truck, trying to get the words out. This whole being open with people thing is a bit rusty for me, but I'm trying to get back to being who I used to be and letting people in.

"Just got done with my therapy session. I'm in a good spot, and I want to win Charlotte back."

Josh breaks out into a huge grin. "Hell yeah, you do! I've been waiting for this day. What do you need my help with?"

"I don't know. I'm not sure what to say. Am I supposed to do some like big grand gesture or something? It feels kind of weird to just approach her and be like, *Hey, I'm not so fucked in the head anymore. Can I get another chance now?*"

He takes time before he responds, which isn't like him. I can tell he's taking this seriously for me. "If I'm being honest, Charlotte doesn't seem like the type to want something too over the top. Something more personal and meaningful seems more like her."

That does sound just like Charlotte. She doesn't want something in front of a crowd or something cheesy. I'm trying to
think of something that's meaningful to her.

Then it dawns on me.

"Oh, I know that face. Did you just think of something?" Josh
smiles.

"I think I've got it."

Chapter Thirty-Two

Charlotte

"How's it going, sweetie?" my mother asks over the phone.

It's a Saturday morning, and I'm just waking up to the sunrise. My coffee is brewing in my new fancy coffee machine.

I'm looking outside as the beautiful colors of the sun begin to peak up over the horizon.

"It's great," I say with a smile. "I'm actually just about to head down to the dock."

"Oh, that was your father's favorite spot," she replies.

Over the last couple of weeks, it's become easier for her to talk about my dad. She was grieving his death in her own way. She even visited a month ago and stayed in my guest bedroom.

It was so nice to have her here. I'm so glad she was able to stay with me, knowing this place is filled with her own memories, whether good or bad.

After I chat with her for a couple of minutes, I grab my coffee and start walking down to the dock. It's October now, so the mornings aren't as warm as they used to be.

I have on my jeans and a baggy sweatshirt.

When I take a seat on the chair, I close my eyes for a moment to enjoy the sounds around me.

As I sip my coffee, my brain floats away to thoughts of Asher as they usually do. I thought if I gave it time, it would get easier.

In some respects, I suppose it has. I'm no longer holding my breath, wondering when or if he'll show up at my door.

But I still think of him every day, and it still hurts when I do.

The heat of the coffee is much-needed to counter the chilliness in the air. I hum my appreciation of the taste as I look out at the boat in the distance.

It's too small to make out what kind of boat it is, but I find myself watching it in fascination as it gets closer.

I'm honestly not much of a boat expert. Most of them look the same to me as they go by. Some of my neighbors have yachts that they park outside their docks, which have always mesmerized me. I used to ask my dad if we could get one, and he would just laugh.

I never understood what was so funny. Now I know they cost millions and that this house was already nearly out of our price range. That's why it always shocked me that he never sold it.

I don't know how he could afford to let it sit here and be such a big asset that was never utilized.

Now, I know it was something that meant a lot to him and that he couldn't part with. Probably for the same reasons I couldn't part with it.

That's weird, the boat seems to be heading right in my direction. I wonder if they are just playing around on the water. Some people like to cut the wheel quickly, going back and forth on the river.

But as the seconds pass, I realize that's not the case.

As soon as the boat is closing in, I spot the driver. My heart drops.

Asher.

What's he doing here?

Oh my god. I can't breathe. I stand up and walk to the side of the dock as his boat slowly pulls into the spot. He wraps the boat rope on the dock after he cuts the engine.

His smirk goes right to my stomach, causing butterflies to take flight.

Then I see Brie sitting on the seat with her life vest on with a lollypop in her mouth. She seems happy as a clam as she watches her dad get the boat tied to the dock.

My eyes sting with tears as I watch her smile up at me through her lollypop.

I didn't realize how much I missed her.

"Morning, beautiful day out, isn't it?" he says nonchalantly.

I think I try to laugh and talk at the same time and end up choking on air. How the hell is he acting so calm? I'm a freakin' mess right now.

"Yeah, beautiful," I finally say on an exhale, knowing it came out all shaky.

He steps back down into the boat and grabs Brie with a bag in his hand. He pulls out what looks like a little bouquet of flowers and hands them to Brie.

As soon as he places her on the dock, he holds her hand as he gets on himself.

I kneel down on the dock to be eye level with Brie. Her sweet blonde hair is up in pigtails on the top of her head and she's wearing strawberry pants and long-sleeve shirt outfit.

It's the cutest thing I've ever seen.

"Daddy say you love strawberries," she says as she points to her outfit.

I smile at her as her chubby little finger starts pointing to several different strawberries along the way. "I do love strawberries! And I love your shirt."

She hands me the flowers that are halfway to the ground since they are almost as big as her body.

"These are so beautiful. Thank you," I reply.

Brie opens her arms and jumps into me. I almost fall backward, but luckily catch myself as I wrap my arms around her.

I stand up with her in my arms, as I finally meet his eyes. He's looking at the two of us together with such admiration it feels like there's no air for me to breathe.

"Care to sit?" he asks as he motions to the chairs.

"Oh, sure," I say as I walk back to the end of the dock.

He pulls a blanket out of his bag and sets up a spot for Brie to sit between our chairs with a snack.

I put her down and she plops onto the blanket as she almost dives for her snack. I chuckle as I watch.

"What are you doing here?" I ask, not sure I can hold back any longer. I need to know.

He looks slightly nervous as he adjusts himself in his seat. He takes a deep breath, like he's preparing himself to speak.

Then he looks at me. "Brie and I have missed you every second of every day that we've been apart."

I didn't expect him to be so direct right off the bat. I don't know how to respond, but my emotions bubble up in my chest, threatening to spill out.

"I couldn't think of a way to say what I wanted to say or do something as big as you deserve," he starts, then he looks out at the water, "then I decided...the only thing that matters was the meaning behind it. And this place, the water, the dock, your house...it holds so much meaning. It's what brought us together again."

He adjusts Brie's water cup that tipped over, ever the multi-tasking father he is. Then he continues, "I used to pass by this dock the last summer you were here on my father's boat, and I remember always looking for you. There was a comfort I would feel when I would spot you sitting out here. I think my body knew even then that you were destined for me. I think part of me loved you back then, I just didn't know it."

Well, now I'm frickin' ugly crying. I try to wipe my tears, but there's no use, and the sounds coming from me must sound terrible. But how could I not when the man I've loved from a distance for so long is telling me he felt the same? That he noticed me at such a deep level even back then.

"These last two months have been so hard to be away from you, even if I knew it was for the best. Still, I couldn't stay away. I would drive my boat by your dock every weekend so I could get a glimpse of you out here. For a brief moment, we were together. Just like it felt all those years ago."

I choke on my tears. "Asher," I whisper.

"I worked really hard with my therapist. And now I'm here hoping, fucking desperately praying, that it's not too late. I'm an open book for you. Ask me anything. I'll tell you anything. My heart is yours. If you'll still have it."

"Daddy loves you," Brie joins in.

I chuckle as tears run down my cheeks. Her interruption was perfect. It's exactly how I pictured my life with him. Never taking life too seriously. "I love your daddy, too," I say.

Brie doesn't seem to hear. She's back to focusing on her food.

But Asher, his attention is all on me. "You still love me?"

I can't help but laugh. "Of course, I still love you. I've missed you two like crazy."

His smile takes up his entire face. It's like the old Asher is back. I can feel it. His energy is different, he seems calm and happy.

"Care to take a ride with us?" Asher asks as he motions toward his boat. "We packed a little breakfast, hoping you would take us back."

"I'd love that."

I lift Brie while Asher packs everything up. I leave my coffee cup behind on the dock, and we jump into the boat. After Brie has her life jacket back on, she sits on my lap while Asher pulls the boat away.

"How did you drive this boat with her here?" I ask, curious about the logistics.

He smiles. "She sat on my lap. I don't trust her to be out of my sight on here. But she seems a lot happier now that you're here."

We both just smile at each other.

Since it hasn't warmed up for the day yet, we don't go too fast while he scouts out a place to drop anchor.

Once he finds his favorite spot, we get everything settled, and he pulls out a thermos with two cups.

"Please tell me there's coffee in there," I plead.

"Of course, there's coffee. There's also probably every pastry you can think of in this box." He pulls out a large pink box from some kind of bakery. "I hate that I don't know your favorites yet, so I got one of everything. But I promise, I will be spending the rest of my life learning everything you like and spoiling you with it."

Swoon. This man. Who would've thought the grumpy, angry man that I reconnected with months ago would turn out to be so sweet and thoughtful?

The rest of the day is perfect. We spent hours out on the boat. Brie took a nap in my arms while we headed back to my dock. Snuggling with her while I watched the sexiest man alive steer the boat with his flexed muscles, it was like a fairytale.

A dirty fairytale where the heroine has very dirty thoughts about the hero.

I haven't felt that man's lips on mine in months, so of course, I'm feeling all kinds of charged up around him.

He did just profess his love for me, too.

Some would say after what we went through, he didn't do enough. I say it was perfect. Bringing along his daughter, meeting me at my favorite spot, sharing his thoughts about watching me when we were younger, it was all I needed.

The truth is, he was always going to have my heart. I trusted and believed him when he said he would work on himself for me.

I know he wanted to get help so he could be better. To me, that's the biggest grand gesture a woman can ask for. A man who is willing to work on himself to be the best man he can be for the woman he loves.

That's a real man. I don't need a flashy moment in front of a crowd. Anybody can do that.

We spend the evening together, making s'mores in his backyard over the firepit. Brie's eyes are nearly rolling in the back of her head as she tries to take down her s'more.

"She is exhausted," I say as we both watch her with amusement. When her face hits her s'more, instead of going into her mouth, I decide it's time to get her in bed. "Alright, I'm taking her to bed. I think she gets a bath tomorrow, right?"

"Yeah," he smiles. "I think she'd have a meltdown if we put her in water right now. I can take her, though, if you want to hang by the fire."

"Not at all," I say as she rests her head on my shoulder. "I want to put her to bed."

As I lie with her and read her a story, my heart feels so full. Her little hand is playing with my hair as her eyelids begin to flutter until they remain closed. I kiss her forehead and tiptoe out of the room, back outside, until I spot Asher outside, still sitting by the fire.

When I open the sliding door, he looks up at me with a smile that makes me feel like the luckiest damn woman in the world.

"Hey, you," he says. "Come here."

He opens his arms, and I don't hesitate to beeline it right into them. In an instant, our lips are on each other's.

The kiss is urgent. It's been months, and it feels like all of the ups and downs are being expressed through this hungry kiss.

He pulls me onto his lap, and we kiss for what feels like an hour. Neither willing to stop. When he finally pulls away, my lips are swollen.

"Damn, I missed you baby," he whispers.

"I missed you."

"Thank you so much for taking me back. I swear, that was last time I will ever need space, from now on, I'm yours. Forever."

The End

Epilogue

Asher

Six Months Later

"Where do you want this?" Josh asks as he balances a large box in his arms.

I look around the house, taking a moment as I reflect on the fact that this is going to be my new home. I never dreamed of living in a place like this.

I turn back around to Josh. "That's Brie's stuff. Her room is the first door on the left upstairs."

"Aye, aye, captain," he jokes as he walks past me.

Ever since I've had Charlotte back in my life, each day has only gotten better. She has become the missing puzzle piece in my life. Her relationship with Brie has turned into something beyond my wildest imagination, and has been everything I wanted for my daughter.

Not only does Charlotte treat her like her own, but she takes the time to talk to her about Lauren. Charlotte understands the importance of remembering that no matter what Lauren did to hurt me, she was first and foremost, the mother of my child.

After doing much research with Charlotte on the topic of post-partum depression, Charlotte is convinced Lauren had it. She doesn't think someone just changes like that after having a baby. Suddenly, needing to get out of the house, leaving their baby with their husband to have an affair. Whether or not that's true, we both agree it's in Brielle's best interest to know how much her mother loved her and will always be with her.

About a month ago, after Charlotte put Brie in bed one night, she asked me what I thought about moving in with her. I already knew I wanted to marry her, so the answer was an obvious one. It just made sense since we were spending every spare minute together.

Now, here we are. A month later, and I'm moving into her childhood home. We are going to create our own memories, and build our own family in her favorite place.

I feel a delicate hand on my lower back. Charlotte's smiling face greets me when I turn around.

"Hey, beautiful," I say as I lean in for a kiss. "Where's Brie?"

"She's running around the backyard with my mom," Charlotte replies. "I don't know why I'm so tired lately, but I told her I needed a bit of a break."

"Well, there's been a lot of stress in the last month. The packing and selling my house. Why don't you go lie down upstairs for a minute?"

I wrap an arm around her then kiss her forehead. I hate to see her feeling sick, but I am a bit concerned. She's been tired a lot lately, and I can see her struggling with it.

After she makes her way upstairs, my brother's come in with more boxes. I spend the rest of the afternoon directing all of them on where it all should go. My mom and Charlotte's mom spend the time occupying Brie. I love how much Charlotte's mother has taken to my daughter. It's like everything has effortlessly fallen into place.

"Daddy!" Brie runs into my arms after I place a box down in the kitchen. I swoop her up and onto my side.

"Hi, sweet pea! You look like you could use a drink."

She nods her head eagerly.

"How's Charlotte feeling?" Leah, Charlotte's mom asks.

I sigh. "She's asleep now. I wonder if she's coming down with the flu."

"Maybe I should run up to the drugstore and get her some medicine."

"That's not a bad idea. It would be nice to have something here on hand for her if she needs it."

Leah grabs her purse and heads out the door. After Brie finishes the drink I gave her, I walk her upstairs and into what is now her new bedroom. In an effort to make sure the transition was as easy as possible for Brie, we ordered all new furniture and let her spend all last week decorating it with us. We even had her take some naps here to get used to it.

So, it comes as no surprise to met when she crawls into her bed and rests her little eyes with comfort and ease.

I sneak out of the room and walk back downstairs where my brothers, and Josh, are gathered in the kitchen.

"Thanks for helping guys. I really appreciate it," I tell them as I join them around the large island.

"Not a problem," Liam replies. "I'm surprised we got it all done so quickly."

"That's because we're strong as fuck," Josh jokes as he flexes.

I roll my eyes but can't contain the laugh. My brother's all look at Josh like a brother, just like I do. He has managed to secure a place in our group with ease.

We all fall into a comfortable silence as I steal a glance outside at the view of the beautiful sun reflecting on the water. It still manages to steal my breath away. I turn back to the guys who seem to be caught up in the same thing.

"Never would've thought you'd be living in a house like this before me," Eric says as he winks. Eric is definitely the most driven out of the three guys.

"Trust me, I never thought I'd live in a house like this *period*."

"I need to find myself a sugar mama like you," Liam jokes.

I punch his arm at his rude statement. The implication, whether a joke or not, is not received well.

"Ouch! What the hell was that for?"

"Don't talk about Charlotte like that. I would never be with her for any reason other than love."

"Calm down. I was just joking," he says while rubbing his arm.

Serves him right. Now he'll think twice before making a comment like that again.

"You wanna have a beer on the deck or something?" Josh suggests.

"I don't know. Charlotte has been feeling a bit off lately. I think it's the flu or stress. I should probably go check on her."

Thankfully, the guys take the hint that I need some time with her. As they all file out the front door, I thank them again for giving up their Saturday to help us move.

Just as I'm shutting the door, Leah walks down the stairs.

"I was just about to go check on her. How's she feeling?" I ask her.

She makes a move to grab her purse in the kitchen before she meets me in the foyer. "She's up now. She's just going to the bathroom. She said she'll meet you outside on the deck when she's done. I'm just going to go rest at the hotel for a bit."

That seems odd. She normally likes to settle down here and visit with us before she goes back to her hotel. She's still easing her way into being back in this house and sleeping in a hotel is helping her take it slow. Either way, if she is tired and wants some space, I don't want to get in the way.

"Well, thanks for all the help with Brie. She had a blast with you."

I lean in for a hug, so grateful for the incredible love she has shown me and my daughter.

"No, problem. She's perfect. You've done a wonderful job with her."

I still choke up at these type of compliments. I'm always terrified that I'm doing the wrong thing when it comes to my daughter.

Once she's gone, I decide a beer on the deck actually sounds good. I grab a cold one from the fridge and sit down outside while I wait for Charlotte to join me.

It's April now, which means the warmer weather is here but it does still get a bit chili at night. Since the sun is still up, the high seventy degrees makes for a perfect temperature after a long day of moving.

With my baby monitor on me, I'm able to relax, knowing that if Brie wakes up and is scared in her new room, I'll be able to get to her in a second.

The back door opens and Charlotte comes out in her sweats. She looks kind of pale which really gets me worried for her. Then I see that she's been crying.

My heart instantly drops into my stomach.

"Baby, are you okay?" I ask as I jump out of my seat.

She nods her head as more tears fall down her cheek. "I'm ok." She looks around the deck. "Can we sit down?"

"Of course." I lead her to the couch where I was seated.

I grab her hands. "What's wrong? Are you not feeling good? Should I get some medicine?"

Her eyes meet mine. She just smiles at me with a strange look in her eyes. I don't know what to make of it.

"I've definitely been feeling off, but I don't think medicine is going to fix it."

"What are you talking about? If we don't have what you need, I'll run out and get something different."

She laughs softly then squeezes my hands. "I should be feeling better in about twelve weeks. At least, that's what all the articles I've read said."

I'm so confused. What kind of flu lasts twelve weeks? Her eyebrows raise suggestively as a smile spread across her face. Then it hits me.

"You're pregnant?" I ask with a whisper.

"I'm pregnant," she responds.

I can't believe it. We haven't been super careful about it, but then again, we haven't been trying. Pregnant? I'm going to have another baby. Brie's going to be a big sister.

My eyes begin to fill with tears. I grab Charlotte's face and lay a kiss on her lips. She laughs as I begin to pepper her with kisses then wrap her up in a hug.

"Are you happy?" she asks.

I pull away. Shocked that she even has to ask. "Happy? I'm thrilled. We're having a baby!"

"I know. I can't believe it. My mom slipped into my room earlier with some pregnancy tests. I would've never thought I was pregnant."

"Damn. I should've thought to do that. I just figured it was stress or the flu."

She chuckles. "Me too. She told me it was exactly how she felt with me. The fatigue that hit her was apparently strong and lasted until the second trimester."

"Wow. Thank goodness your mom was here. How are you feeling now?" I ask, peeking down at her belly like I'm suddenly going to see a bump there.

"Still a bit weak and tired, but definitely better than before. I could use some food."

Right. Food. She's eating for two now.

"Does Italian sound good?" I ask, remembering Lauren craved heavy carbs while pregnant.

Charlotte moans at the thought. "Yes, Italian sounds wonderful."

Before I can even think about ordering the food, I open my arms to her. "Come here. I need to hold you first."

She smiles and falls into my arms willingly, resting her head on my chest. We lean back into the back of the couch as I enjoy the feeling of her warmth on me.

"Can you believe it?" she whispers into my chest. "This is our life. How lucky are we?"

I just hold her tighter.

I can't believe this is my life. Just a year ago, I was stuck in so much grief and anger that I would have never thought it was possible to find happiness again.

It's incredible how one person can come into your life and turn it all upside down. From the moment that she came back, it was like I could breathe again. Now, here we are sitting on our deck with the most incredible three-year-old upstairs, and a little one growing in her belly.

I don't know what I did to deserve this second chance at love, but I know I will never take it for granted. I will appreciate every moment, every kiss, and every stumble along the way. It will be nothing like the last time, because this time, I'm going to appreciate the time we have together, because all of it is a gift.

Also by Nicole Baker

<u>THE BRADY SERIES</u>
<u>Enough</u>
<u>Impossible</u>
<u>Irresistible</u>
<u>Persuade</u>
<u>Protected</u>

<u>THE GIANNELLI SERIES-LOVE IN LITTLE ITALY</u>
<u>Where You Belong</u>
<u>Where We Met</u>
<u>Where We Fall</u>

<u>ISLE OF HOPE SERIES</u>
<u>The Last Time</u>

Follow Me on Social Media

To have access to my bonus scenes– visit my website and subscribe to my newsletter. You will be directed to a special page on my website with ALL bonus scenes.

www.nicolebakerauthor.com

Follow me for exclusive news on releases, signings, and giveaways.

Facebook @nicolebakerauthor

Instagram @nicolebaker_author

TikTok @authornicolebaker